MW01106533

What Comes From Within

SONAL BAWA BAKSHI

EDITED BY
VINCENT VARGHESE

About the Book

"Those who don't own their life,
end up getting owned by someone else."

Nisha looked forward to a life filled with dreams coming true, until one day, her immigrant parents get killed in a car crash and she's left orphaned at ten in Vancouver, Canada.

With no friends or relatives who can take her in, she is put through one foster home after another, facing abuse, until all she is left with is a will to survive and the undying love and loyalty of her only friend, Carol.

Toughened by the unending trauma and no real future to look forward to, Nisha grows up into a fiercely determined and headstrong woman who makes it her life's purpose to avenge the murder of her parents by destroying the man who killed them and ended her dreams. Does she succeed? What is the cost of her revenge?

Will Nisha be able to live the life she dreamt of? Will she know love and happiness in the shadow of revenge? A daring debut novel by Sonal Bawa Bakshi, "What Comes From Within" is a thrilling ride from start to finish.

A plot that fills you with nervous excitement, an unpredictable bold character and a twist in every chapter – this book has it all – Love, Passion, Revenge, Betrayal and Survival. The best modern revenge thriller you can lay your hands on this year.

Published by Destiny Media LLP 2022

Website: www.destinymedia.in

Cover Design: Patanjali Sharma

ISBN

Hardcover: 978-81-952172-7-4

Paperback: 978-81-952172-6-7

E-Book: 978-81-952172-8-1

Dedication

"Behind every successful woman, is a tribe of other successful women who have her back."

This book is dedicated to all the strong matriarchs who raised me to be fearless, strong and independent just like them.

"Not a day goes by when I don't miss you, but I know you're always there smiling and guiding me - till we meet again."

This book is also dedicated to my late father who not only celebrated my success but also comforted me in my failures.

A man of few words, he, in his own way taught me to be confident in everything I did.

What Comes From Within

Chapter One

It's 9 pm on a cold winter evening.

We are three weeks away from Christmas and the entire city of Vancouver is decked out in festive lights. It is -5 F and the snow is coming in thick and fast, refusing to stop. It's been snowing for the past 48 hours and the whole city is covered in a blanket of snow.

I shove my hands deeper into the pockets of my jacket as I hide in the darkness behind a wall. I look like a gangster, dressed in baggy khakis, a hoodie, a baseball cap and a heavy jacket.

I notice the swanky new Tesla pulling into the office building. The Monster is here.

A big, grey haired man with a salt and pepper beard gets out and walks into the building. He struts about like he owns the building. Well, he does own it...

Shiv Patel, real estate tycoon, stalwart of the industry, winner of many awards and citations. Seeing him walk in fills me with an anger I can barely control. And yet, I must stay calm and think. What should I do? Should I go ahead with the plan? Or should I wait for a better day? I pull the hoodie in over my head, almost covering my eyes. I look around me to see if there is anything else I should be worried about. No, nothing!

The world looks exactly like it's meant to – unconcerned and too obsessed with itself to bother about anyone else. Everyone talks a lot, but does nothing about the things that really matter. It's almost as if everything is done only for social media - for yet another pretty Instagram post.

Christmas will come soon. And after that, another year will begin. And life will go on in an endless repetition. Monsters will do whatever they want and innocents will struggle to cope with their devastation. No one will care. As long as the victims keep quiet, no one will pay attention. No, not this time. Not me. I won't be silenced. I will fight back. I will have my revenge. Even if it costs me my life. And I will win. Because no one else is willing to give up as much of themselves as me. So here goes.

I rotate my shoulders to get some blood flowing. Take a few deep breaths, grit my teeth and bend my head as I walk towards Variety Real Estate's office building.

I walk through the heavy, big glass doors into a huge marble lobby with a tall celling and massive granite pillars. Huge planters with ferns and other tall plants adorn the open marble lobby. A couple of orange and red arm chairs and couches do a decent job of adding colour to the otherwise white and grey space. I try to hang around waiting for someone to get into the elevator so that I can tailgate.

"Hey, are you waiting for someone?"

A guard approaches me with a suspicious look on his face, one hand on the baton hanging by his hip and the other on the talkie resting on his shoulder. I've already anticipated this. I turn away from the surveillance camera that I've noticed while walking in, pull off the hoodie revealing long curly blonde hair and give him the sweetest smile any girl could've given to get her way.

"I.... It's cold out there...so I thought I'd sit here for a while, just to warm myself. I'll leave if you want me to."

He comes closer; the suspicious look gives way to a warm smile.

"You're welcome to sit here. If you want, there is a cafeteria on the 10th floor where you can get warm coffee or hot chocolate." He clicks his tongue and winks as he leaves me alone.

As soon as he's out of sight, the hoodie comes back over my head and the gangster is back. I shove my hands in my pockets and casually walk towards the elevator as I join the janitor riding to the 23rd floor.

The elevator doors open on to what is a huge reception area with tiled floors, large slanting windows, colourful couches and vibrant art work adorning the dove grey walls. It is very quiet with dimmed lights and empty corridors as the staff have left for the day. I use that to my advantage as I hide in the shadows from a security guard patrolling the office. There is only one light in a large corner office that catches my eye and as I'm about to go there, my phone buzzes. I curse under my breath and hurriedly pull it out. The screen flashes: CAROL.

I try to ignore it, but like a stubborn child it persists forcing me to take the call.

"WHAT?" I whisper impatiently.

"Nal, are you in?"

"Yes!" I whisper, almost scolding her!

"Whatever you do, don't get caught."

"Like I don't know!" I reply sarcastically and end the call.

I hurriedly put the phone away and like a cheetah on a hunt, I am back to the business at hand.

I make a quiet but swift entry into Shiv Patel's huge corner office. The office is dimly lit by a floor lamp standing in one corner of the room and a lone laptop sitting on a huge work desk that is cluttered with paper. I cautiously walk around the table and sit on the floor... looking around, taking it all in.

Monsters and predators get to own million-dollar office buildings and swanky corner offices, while the people they prey on have to make do with the crumbs that society throws at them, often out of pity or guilt.

No one seems to be around. I don't know where Shiv Patel went.

Which means, he could be here any moment. I better hurry.

I open the laptop on the table and bring it to life, then plug my tiny almost invisible thumb drive into it. The software loads on its own, and a small window appears - "Copying files!"

Now the most difficult part begins.

Waiting!

I hold my breath as I watch the files being transferred slowly into my thumb drive: 1%... 10%... 30%...

With every passing minute, my heart pounds faster and louder. I cross my fingers and say a silent prayer. If there is a God, he'll get me through this.

Just then the booming voice of Shiv Patel gets closer...

"I don't care, I want the deal closed. Give them what they want and GET IT DONE!"

I cringe as I see the shadow of the tall well-built man walking towards the corner office while talking on the phone. He looks like a 250-pound hulk who could easily strangle me to death if he wanted to. Loud, curt with a deep scratchy voice and a dismissive air about him - an alpha male with a dominant demeanour that makes me really nervous. My heart is pounding faster now.

I shut the laptop, squat down and hide under the table, holding my breath.

I hear him come into the cabin and stand close to where I'm hiding.

"Please, please." I pray silently as I crawl away towards the side of table to avoid getting noticed. My heart is pounding louder against my chest and I press down on it, in an attempt to calm down.

"You understand that this is an important deal. I don't fucking care about your problems. Get this approved now or you're out of Variety."

I dare a peak now from behind the table and see him pick up a bunch of files and walk out of the room again.

In an instant, I'm back up at the laptop. I open it up again.

The copying seems to have been frozen first at 65%, then at 80%...

"Hurry up, please." I whisper as if talking to someone beside me. Sweat trickles down my forehead and between my breasts, making me want to wipe it away.

I hunch over the laptop, wishing I could do something to make it work faster.

"I have spoken to the mortgage broker about the ratios and he's told me that the numbers are in line. I'll send you the details of the deal soon."

I hurriedly duck down again as I see Shiv coming back into the cabin, a couple of files under his arm.

Oh God! I've forgotten to shut the laptop!

He stops at the door and scans the room; almost as if he's seen me.

I freeze and stop breathing.

He keeps looking around taking in every square inch of the room.

I'm hoping that he won't see me hiding in the darkness.

He notices the laptop, looks at the screensaver on it, then shuts it, turns off the light, picks up the keys on his desk and walks out.

I wait for a few minutes, just to make sure that he's actually gone and then cautiously come out from the darkness and open up the laptop. The download is finally complete. I hurriedly take the thumb drive out of the laptop, shove it in my pocket and leave the now pitch-dark office.

As soon as I step out of Shiv Patel's office, the alarm bells start screaming away... have I been spotted? Fuck, I better get out of here alive. I run as fast as I can and push open the fire exit and run down the stairs... I hear someone shout at a distance...

"He's definitely in the building, find the intruder NOW!"

As I'm hurtling down the stairs, I keep my eyes and ears wide open to pick up any sign of where the security guards are moving towards.

Seems like fate is not on my side today, I hear dogs barking below and voices of men screaming and scrambling to find the intruder...me!

As I rush down the stairs trying hard not to panic, I hear a growl and stop to look back. Standing just a few feet away from me is a huge Alsatian, growling ferociously, spit drooling from its mouth. "Stay calm, stay focused, and move slowly." I autosuggest as I scan around, my brain working overtime to somehow get out alive!

The dog stretches into an attack position and I run as fast as my legs carry me, sliding down the rail from time to time. A few flights down, I see the exit door and I jump from the fifth step. I twist my ankle and continue running despite the excruciating pain.

My next hurdle is getting past the spiked gate that leads to a dark alley at the back of the building. I hurriedly step up on to the gate and as I climb over the spikes, my leg gets stuck. To make matters worse, I have that same dog now jumping up to bite me. I kick the dog as hard as I can and somehow manage to free my leg but end up hurting myself badly. I clamber down the other side, with a twisted ankle, a badly bleeding leg and run ahead to save my life. My heart is racing faster than my feet, the adrenaline rushing through my veins; I've been running non-stop for what feels like an hour. Today I did something that I would normally never do and I'm ecstatic, because I have been able to get a hold of Shiv Patel's laptop. I know that this will change the course of my life.

I rush towards the car parked next to the huge dumpster and jump into it. I struggle to put on the seat belt while Carol concentrates on speeding away from the scene.

Yeah Carol.

Life-saver-Carol.

Hysterical-anxiety-prone-techie-Carol.

Damsel-in-distress-when-she-wants-to-be-Carol.

If-you-fuck-with-my-sister-I'll-cut-your-dick-off-Carol.

My BFF - my sister - my confidante all-rolled-into-one Carol.

"Are you out of your fucking mind, what the fuck is wrong with you?" Carol tries to examine my leg while keeping an eye on the road.

I'm smiling from ear to ear as I wonder...

"Should we go to the nearest walk in clinic and get a dressing done."

Carol screams back "NO, if you go to a clinic or a hospital, the security guards can track you down and it will be used as evidence."

I nod in agreement as Carol drives frantically through the snow to get me home.

After 45 minutes, we reach home. I limp hurriedly, ignoring the pain in my leg and Carol's constant nagging.

"I told you to be careful! What if the guards had caught you? That would have been the end of you!"

I pull out the thumb drive from my pocket, hands shaking with the cold and nervous exhilaration.

Carol hands me a glass of wine and stands next to me, staring as the laptop screen comes to life.

"So, what do we have here?"

She takes a sip and gestures me to take one too.

I turn to her, eyes wide with excitement.

"This, my friend, is the first attack in bringing down Shiv Patel!"

I gulp down the glass of wine, wipe my mouth with the back of my hand and once again start clattering on the keyboard while standing on one leg.

"No, no, not happening. You have the entire night and the whole day tomorrow to go through your treasure."

She pulls me away and makes me sit on the couch, feet up on a stool. She sits in front of me, ready with antiseptic, some bandages and Band-Aids.

"Take an Advil or Tylenol for the pain." She instructs as she cleans the wound and applies antiseptic cream, and I like an obedient child, take the painkiller and sit quietly watching my leg get bandaged.

I look at Carol and think of how much she means to me. She's my mother and my sister all rolled into one. Short, strong willed with a scary IQ, Carol is the best thing that has happened to me in this life.

Behind all that nervousness and anxiety is a fierce tech warrior who can seriously out think most computer wizards.

I smile to myself as she finishes up and instructs me to get to bed. She notices me looking at her.

"What?!"

"Thank you!" I hug her.

Carol hugs me back "It's only just begun. You have to stop being so impulsive!"

I'VE BEEN UP on the thumb drive the whole night, polished off a big bottle of Merlot, scanned each and every document. A lot of Shiv Patel's personal life is now lying exposed in front of me - his net worth, his debts, who he paid off and the amount of each transaction. It's stunning how much private information our laptops hide for us.

I smile to myself knowing that I have an advantage over Shiv Patel – not something you come across very easily.

"Looks like you could definitely use some coffee."

Carol walks across into the kitchen, wearing shorts and a spaghetti top. I snap out of my thoughts and look around. The apartment is warm and cozy with sunlight streaming through the windows, making the place bright and comfy.

"Come here quickly, I have something to show you; coffee can wait."

I am excited and can't wait to share it with her. She opens the fridge, takes out a bottle of water smiling and shaking her head,

"Hold your horses, lady. We can go through the documents over coffee and muffins."

I lie down, soaking in the sun, as I wait for her to make coffee and warm some muffins. "There you go, my love." I gratefully take the steaming cup of coffee as Carol settles next me.

Together, we go through the documents outlining Shiv's offshore accounts, his personal debts and liabilities.

"This is just the start, I've kept the best for the last." I wink at her as I scroll to the next document; Variety's new projects; Company bank account details, how much money is in the demand accounts.

Carol seems to have gone into shock as she continues to drink her coffee while occasionally nibbling on her muffin. I playfully nudge her, "now comes the fun part, so brace yourself."

I put the laptop aside and face her.

"Shiv Patel has a mistress for the last three years, he pays the mortgage for a penthouse in West Van through an account that no one in his family or his company, know of." Carol looks surprised. I open a folder on the thumb drive.

Nude pictures of a stunningly beautiful woman taken from a mobile phone pop up on screen. Carol lets out a small whistle. I laugh as I see the expression on her face.

Carol looks like she's popped a few CBD gummies; zoned out and is now speechless.

The woman on the screen is a picture-perfect blond with a great body. Spotless, fair, baby soft skin and silky hair falling perfectly on to her shoulders.

Carol whistles again as she sees the photo, "Shiv is one lucky bastard."

In today's day and age, it is not hard to find someone online and especially if that someone is a hot, sexy, super model type. Carol immediately grabs the computer and within a minute manages to pull out every detail on our little missy with her perfect figure. Her reverse image search yields a result.

"Hey, look at this; our little miss perfect everything is none other than Miss Victoria 1st runner up, Stephanie Milton. After she lost to... what's that other chick's name?"

I snap my fingers trying to remember, "Adrianne?"

Carol sounded and looked unsure, "That's it.... So, when she lost that pageant, she disappeared from the scene all together, never to be seen or heard about again and for the longest time. It was rumoured that she had moved out to a European country. Who would've thought that she was actually living the secret life of 'I'm-the-one-screwing-the-millionaire?'"

"Carol, we need to get more information on this chick, she can be our key to a lot of other secrets that that bastard Shiv has."

Both of us stare at the social media images of our next target - Stephanie Milton.

Chapter Two

It's 11 am and we've been parked for over an hour outside the sea facing apartment building, home to Shiv Patel's newly discovered mistress.

I'm itching to get out of the car to scout further but Carol stops me.

She looks at me, takes a sip of her coffee and chuckles, "Darling, you need to understand that we are not up against someone from the streets, this is Shiv Patel, the business tycoon. Someone who is known as the Real Estate Giant of Canada. So, for once, you need to calm down and think it through to the end. Irrational, reckless behaviour now can ruin everything!"

I turn away, look outside the car and sulk. Carol has always been upfront and brutally honest with me, whether I like it or not.

We sit listening to Queen's 'We will Rock you' on 103.5 QM FM and sipping on hot coffee.

"Looks like we'll be getting more snow, so brace yourselves, Vancouver, it is going to be a snowy white weekend... And now, here's Maroon 5's 'Girls Like You', enjoy" says the cheerful voice of the RJ.

"God, I love his.... OMG!!! It's her, that's her." I almost

scream as I whip out my phone and zoom to the max to take the photo of the gorgeous Stephanie Milton.

I chuckle and take a sip of what was supposed to be a hot cappuccino but has converted itself into cold caffeine flavoured water as Carol looks at the photos.

"Nal, it's time to go. We got what we were looking for, there's nothing much we can do at this time. Let's go home and work out a plan."

I pop a gum, chew for a few seconds, blow a bubble and POP.

"Nope, not yet, as per Shiv's email, she's supposed to get a special 'cash' delivery and I want to see who our delivery person is."

Carol sighs as she pushes her seat back into a recliner position and puts her hands behind her head.

An hour later a red Tesla turns into the parking lot of the building.

I pull out my phone and zoom in.

As I had suspected, it was driven by a young, 20 something immaculately dressed guy in a formal suit, wearing Tom Ford glasses.

Before I can say anything though, Carol has already stepped out of the car and is heading towards the apartment, holding her phone as if she's doing Face Time while smoking a cigarette.

Twenty minutes later, she comes back with tons of photos and without wasting time, we reverse image search the guy.

"Our mystery man is Edward McPherson working for Variety Real Estate."

Carol whistles as she reads about him on social media.

"He's been with the company for almost a year and has been trying to move up in the company, which is why he does anything and everything that Shiv asks him to, in other words, he is Shiv's sidekick and confidante."

"Now that explains the money."

We see Edward McPherson leaving in his swanky car with Stephanie seeing him off.

As soon he leaves, I put on my baseball cap and kiss Carol on the cheek, "Wish me luck, hun, I'm gonna go and get her."

I don't wait for her response, jump out of the car and head towards the apartment building with a phone in one hand and my laptop in the other.

I get into the lift with her and follow her to her apartment door.

"Can I help you?"

I hate to admit it but she's prettier than her pictures and maybe it's showing on my face as she scowls and impatiently taps her feet.

It could be my checkered past or even the kind of life I've lived, but I always envy a beautiful, naïve girl living a protected secure life.

If I could have traded a year of my life so far, for even a day of her manicured life, I would take the deal without thinking!

Meanwhile, this naïve beautiful girl looks at me with attitude in her eyes.

I gather myself and spcak slowly and confidently.

"I've come to warn you about Shiv Patel, I have evidence that he's just using you. He will dump you very soon as he's already flirting with another, younger girl."

"That's not possible, Shiv loves me and has promised to marry me and make me a partner in his firm. In fact, he's opening another office in Italy and sending me there to head operations."

I can't help but laugh at her. She gets really pissed off and looks at me angrily.

As she begins to start talking, I calmly open up some photos on my phone and show them to her.

Stephanie reluctantly looks at a photo of a really beautiful 19 something model type girl taking a selfie with Shiv Patel.

Stephanie looks as if she's been punched in the gut, eyes filled with tears and shaking her head in denial.

"Hun, all ok? Who is this girl?"

A man, in his mid-70's, walks out from the apartment opposite Stephanie's looking both curious and suspicious.

Stephanie much to my surprise recovers quickly.

"Hi Doug, yeah all's well. This is my friend; she was in the neighbourhood and just stopped by to meet me. Have a great day"

She hurriedly ushers me into her gorgeous apartment. As I walk in, I look around.

It has a huge living room with white leather couches, a white and grey plush carpet with a low coffee table in the middle, a huge fireplace and a couple of palms in big pots.

The room is very airy with lots of light; thanks to the tall windows and the French door leading to a big patio overlooking the Pacific Ocean and the snowcapped mountains.

I walk towards the tall French door, hands in my back pocket.

"Wow, I'd sleep with a 60-year-old fart any day to have one of these." I say out loud.

Stephanie looks irritated. "What's your name?"

I feel sorry for her but I have to walk the straight and narrow.

I need to get her to do what I want.

"Get me a coffee and I'll tell you!"

I go back to looking at the view wondering if my gamble will work out. She seems like a nice girl but...

"Here's your coffee."

Stephanie walks in holding two cups of steaming coffee, puts one on the table and sits on the love seat opposite the four-seater couch. I take a quick picture of the view and sit across from her.

"So, where were we?"

I turn on my laptop and turn it towards her, "see this, these are the screen shots of Shiv's emails and this one here, read it, he's going to New York for the Victoria Secret fashion show next weekend and will be spending time with the girl whose selfie I showed you."

She looks shocked and appalled.

Before I can figure out whether she's angry with me or angry with herself for being so foolish, she blurts out in tears "who the FUCK are you and what the FUCK do you want?"

That's it! I'm in the game!

I sit back, cross my leg, put an arm on the back of the couch in a Godfather pose.

"Well, I'll offer you a deal: you co-operate with me and I will get you the Villa that Shiv has just bought, along with a million dollars."

Stephanie is taken aback. She stares at me with her mouth half open.

I lean in. "My name is Nalini and I want Shiv to pay for what he's done. To you. And to me!"

She leans back, squints as she looks at me, "and why should I trust you?"

I give her a smile that says you're so naïve, "because you've seen me and you can turn me in and press charges against me."

Before she can figure out what to do next...

"Go ahead, take a photo of me! That way you'll have your proof that I came to meet you with this offer."

She picks up her phone and takes my photo.

"Good. Now that you have your proof, let me continue. You don't really have a choice. You will have to do whatever I ask you to do. I have pictures of you taking money from Edward. I can prove that Shiv is using you and paying you money every month. I can put this all over the media. And you know how these kinds of scandals play out."

Stephanie looks lost and abandoned. She looks like she would start weeping helplessly.

I feel sorry for her and put a hand on her shoulder.

"I'm not your enemy Stephanie. Shiv is! He's the one using you. Take my offer. Take your million dollars, take your villa and get the fuck out of his life. That's the best of what you're going to get from him. You're young and smart. You don't have to get used like this. Take my offer because it's the best one you'll ever get. Do you understand?!"

Stephanie looks lost for a long moment. Then wipes off her tears, looks at me and nods.

Then in a grief filled voice she mumbles, "What do you want me to do?"

Carol anxiously taps her cell phone between her fingers as she gazes at Stephanie's apartment window.

"Damn it, Nal, come back."

She puts the phone on speaker and dials Nal's number only to get her voicemail.

She disconnects swearing loudly, "damn it, what the fuck."

She throws the phone on the seat next to her and runs her hand through her hair, then looks up and is horrified to see a cop car pull up beside their car.

A young, well-built constable steps out and looks at her curiously.

She smiles and steps out of the car.

"Are you here to meet someone?"

He walks around her car checking the interiors and looking suspiciously at her.

Carol puts on her best I'm-just-an-innocent-damsel-looking-for-some-fun face and says, "Well, I'm here to enjoy the view. What is a good-looking cop like you doing here? Surely, you're not here just to check out an innocent girl, or are you?"

She stands close to him and gives him her favourite I'm-so-into-you smile.

The cop looks like he's forgotten what he was doing.

She ever-so-innocently puts her hand on his chest.

He smiles, then quickly remembers what he was supposed to be doing and pushes her hand away.

"I'm on duty, so I cannot... again, what are you doing here?"

"So, can I have your number and maybe we'll meet for drinks over the weekend and then I can tell you all about it." Carol says huskily.

The cop can't believe he's lucked out. He writes his number on the ticket and hands it over before leaving.

Carol starts feeding his number into her phone and then looks up to find Nal looking at her. Startled, Carol almost jumps away.

"What's up?" I ask her casually.

"What the fuck is wrong with you? Why would you not take my calls?" Carol starts yelling and pacing nonstop rubbing her hands; something that she does when she is nervous.

I put my laptop on the backseat, then look at Carol who is still processing her emotions. Carol walks up to me and says in a 'I – MEAN – BUSINESS' tone.

"Nal, there was a cop patrolling the area and I thought that that fucking bitch had called him on us. Had I not flirted with him, we would be charged with trespassing and threatening a citizen."

I hug her.

"We have her!"

It's now Carol's turn to look surprised.

"Say what... You're serious? Does she know..."

"She's in. She'll do whatever we want in exchange for that villa and a million dollars. I gave her a dignified way to get out of a toxic relationship and she took it. She's a smart girl."

Carol looks at me stunned. "You did... what?"

THE SNOW HAS ALMOST MELTED NOW and it has become a fairly warm day for winter.

Carol sits on the laptop, typing away furiously... while I bring a couple of steaming hot coffees and muffins. Carol is mumbling away nervously even as she types furiously.

"How's it going?" I ask. Just to calm her nerves.

Carol mumbles... "I've downloaded all the photos from her account and am creating a fake profile. Let's see how quickly I can create a credible one."

I smile knowing that this anxiety-ridden-short-white-super-smart-sister-of-mine will come through in the end.

Our lives have always been filled with challenges and yet the one thing that has been consistent is our love for each other. Carol is the only person I give a fuck about in this world.

The only person I would die or kill for.

I see Edward come out of his red Tesla and look around for us, "there he is, come on Carol, hurry up."

Carol finally presses the enter button and smiles to herself. "Boom-boom-boom! And it's done!"

Carol and I high five each other!

I get up and walk out of the warm café onto the beach while Carol keeps sitting there, biting into her muffin, staring at the laptop!

I notice Edward McPherson walking about on the beach looking for us.

I rotate my shoulders, take a few deep breaths, calm myself and walk up to him

"Hi Edward, thanks for coming out on such short notice."

Edward looks at me moving his eyes all over then looks up at my face. "No gun on me. I promise!"

I smile with the confidence of a girl who knows that she's got the man by the balls.

"Cut the crap and come to the point, what the fuck do you want from me?"

I gesture to him to move towards a nearby bench, it is 2 Degree F but with the sun, it feels like 10!

"Let's sit and talk, shall we?"

"So, who the hell are you and what do you want from me?" He is clearly upset and paces across, hands in his pockets.

"For starters, who I am isn't important, what I can do for you is. And that comes at a price."

He refuses to sit. Stands in front of me, as if trying to intimidate me, crosses his hands across his chest and scowls, "What do you want?"

"I know that you're planning on proposing to your girlfriend and have been looking at properties." He stares at me with disbelief.

"It does not end here, I also know that you were caught cheating with an old classmate of yours, by your girlfriend, which is why she does not trust you."

His expression changes.

From fake confidence to serious concern.

I raise my eyebrows and smile at him.

"I also know that you've been siphoning off cash from your company accounts and using that to buy gifts for your girlfriend to convince her to marry you!"

"What the fuck?! How do you..."

"If you get me what I want, not only will I give you a $1,000; I will also put in a good word for you to your girlfriend and her family. Your call."

I shrug my shoulders and look away as if I didn't care what he does next.

Edward turns red and runs his hand through his hair as he walks away taking deep breaths and exhaling loudly.

He comes back, face flushed, looking even more nervous and clears his throat.

"I need to know, how, ummm, how do you know all this and...."

"How I know this is irrelevant Edward. If it comes down to it, I can prove it in court. That's what matters."

"But..."

"I have your girlfriend's email from her Facebook profile and I can make up a fake email address and shoot her one from the girl you cheated with... your ex. In that email your ex will apologize to your girlfriend for all the allegations and the rumours she had spread about you. She will vouch for your good character. She will also confess that she seduced you because she didn't want to lose you! You know... coz you're a nice guy and all that. But now she's had a change of heart and she does not want to ruin your life and promises to never have anything to do with you ever again."

He looks overwhelmed and quietly mumbles.

"What do you want from me in return?"

I stand and walk up to him.

"I want all the bank statements of all Variety's accounts for the last five years. I also need the details of slush fund accounts from where you pay Stephanie."

Edward once again runs his hands through his hair and walks around with both his hands on his head.

"What the fuck, do you even know what you're saying, can you hear yourself and I don't know any Stephanie."

I go closer to him, close enough to smell the cologne and see a bead of sweat on his forehead. I open up the photo of him paying Stephanie and show it to him.

He takes a step back knowing that he's in real trouble. I step away from him, letting him inhale deeply and curse under his breath.

"Is it just the statements that you're looking for or something else?"

His tone is rushed as if he wants to end the conversation and get out of here.

"I need all official and unofficial statements of all the accounts and I will in turn fulfil my promise of paying you and convincing your girlfriend to marry you. Once you've given me what I want, it'll be like this conversation never happened. No one will ever come to know about our deal."

He still does not look convinced but knows that there is nothing he can do.

"Are we on the same page?"

Edward struggles to think clearly.

I call Carol, a missed call from my phone.

Within a second, Edward gets an email from the fake ID we've created for his ex.

Edward looks at it. It's got photos of them together with just one sentence. "I miss you. I want you back!"

Edward looks like he's about to get run over by a bus.

20

Seconds later, he gets another email where his ex apologises to his current girlfriend for messing up their life, just like the one I'd described to him.

Edward looks at the second email then again at me.

I place a hand on his shoulder, "I know it is hard but you don't have a choice other than to do as I say."

Edward takes a deep breath. "Okay, I'll do it. I'll get you all the statements!"

I pat him on his shoulder. "Good choice...meet me in P2 of your apartment parking lot at 8.30 tonight with all the documents and tomorrow onwards, your life will change for the better! I promise!"

I pat his cheek and walk back to the café, leaving him staring into the sand with his mouth wide open.

SHIV PATEL LOOKS at the security footage of the intruder.

He stares at the blurred image of what seems like a blonde girl showing her face to the security guard before taking the lift.

"Is that a man or a woman?"

The security manager rewinds the footage again. Both of them look at it again.

"Looking at the walk, I think it's a woman."

Shiv nods. They try to zoom onto the face, but it's not visible at all.

"She's about five foot six with blonde hair! That's all we can see from this angle."

Shiv keeps staring at the monitor trying to get a glimpse of the face but can't. He grits his teeth. "Tell the security guard to help us reconstruct the face of the person he allowed into the building. And once he's done with that, fire him!"

The security manager nods.

"And if this ever happens again, you'll go next." The manager squirms.

"And get me an image of the girl based on the security guard's description immediately!"

"Yes Sir!"

Shiv pounds his fist into the table and walks away mumbling... "Fucking idiots!"

CAROL LOOKS at the file that Edward has just given us.

She puts her mobile flashlight on... then shuffles through the papers while I drive us back home.

"It's all there! You can easily take down Shiv Patel with all the info you have now!"

"No! This is just the beginning. We have to get inside his head. We have to destroy him and his company from within. That's the only way the likes of Shiv Patel get destroyed."

Carol looks at me in horror.

"What are you trying to do Nal? You have all the information you need, all the documents, all the frauds and the bribes, everything! You have enough to destroy Shiv Patel for life."

I smile and look out of the window.

"I want Shiv Patel dead! That's the only way this ends."

My phone buzzes with an email that brings a big wide smile to my face.

Carol looks really concerned. "What is it?"

"Looks like even the heavens are on my side for once."

I show Carol the email from Variety confirming my interview for the job I applied for, tomorrow morning.

She looks at me, pale with fear. I pat her hand.

"Don't worry Carol. We will win and everything will be fine. Just be there..."

"I will always be there for you Nal. You're all I have!"

I put my hand on hers and take a deep breath.

"Someday soon, when all of this is over, we'll get our life back. I promise!"

Chapter Three

S hiv look at the coloured sketch drawn up by a sketch artist based on the description given by the security guard. He keeps staring at the image of the young woman in the picture as if he's seen her somewhere. He can't quite place her correctly, but she looks somewhat familiar.

Meanwhile the tech guy who is looking at his computer finally gives up.

"It doesn't make sense Sir!"

"What?"

"Not a single file is out of place! There's no software download or upload. No bugs, no malware, no spy app, nothing! It's like a ghost has been through your laptop. I can't find anything!"

"How is that possible? I know that this woman entered this room and nothing else has been stolen. So, what was she doing here?"

The tech guy looks at him confused.

"Get out!"

As the tech guy leaves, Shiv stares at the sketch of the girl on his table and puts a paperweight on it.

❇

I WALK through the same huge revolving glass doors into the massive lobby with plain white tile floors, tall, sturdy pillars touching the vast ceiling and big slanting glass windows that let the sunlight stream in making the place bright and cheerful.

The place looks different, alive during the day, with the buzz of people walking around, the sound of the phone ringing at the corner reception desk with a bored young receptionist chewing gum as she stares blankly at the computer screen in front of her.

I walk up to her and softly say, "Hi, I have an interview at Variety Real Estate at 10 am today."

She continues to stare at her computer screen and chew on the gum that must've become stale in her mouth by now. I stand there for another couple of minutes and tap my foot impatiently as I watch her pull out the gum out of her mouth as a long strand and then slowly put it back in.

I clear my throat in an attempt to get her attention but she acts as if I don't exist and continues to just sit and stare blankly at the screen.

I then slam my folder in frustration on the reception desk, she jumps from her seat and looks straight at me with confusion in her eyes, "may I help you?" she casually removes her Jabra noise canceling ear phones, sighs and gives me the most disinterested look ever.

I give a sarcastic smile, "sorry to disturb you, but I have an interview at Variety Real Estate office – which way?" I raise my eyebrows and sigh with frustration as she continues to look at me blankly – I'm already running late and this young unambitious girl with her stale chewing gum and her fancy noise cancelling earphones is not making anything better.

She rolls her eyes and points towards four elevators in the semi lit hallway, "take any one of them and it'll take you to 23rd floor – Variety's office."

As I turn towards the elevators, I suddenly hear a familiar growl from just behind me. I turn back and see the same Alsatian dog standing right behind me.

Panic overwhelms me as I suddenly remember coming close to being mauled to death by it a little over 24 hours ago. I just stand still staring at the dog as it moves into attack position.

The dog keeps barking furiously. I suppose it's mad at me for kicking it really hard. And it remembers my smell. Before I can think or figure out what to do in this completely unexpected situation, the dog leaps at me grabbing my trousers between its sharp teeth. Completely taken by surprise and fearful for my life, I let out a scream...

"Someone please help! This dog is about to..."

"Bruno! Stay!"

The soothing calming voice of a man booms out from far away. I struggle to hold on to my trousers before the dog tears it apart. A handsome young man walks towards us. He grabs the dog's leash and yanks it away. The dog keeps barking loudly. The man physically pulls the dog away.

Meanwhile the security guards come rushing in and grab the dog from the man and take it away. I don't know why, but I just burst into tears. The man looks at me sympathetically...

"I'm sorry, this dog, Bruno is particularly aggressive. Something must have triggered him!"

He grabs my hand and gently pulls me towards a chair.

I sit and focus on controlling my breathing.

Breathe in. Overcome your fear.

Breathe out. Forget about this incident.

Breathe in. You are here for an interview.

Breathe out. Focus on what you came here for.

Within a few seconds, I regain my composure. I finally overcome my panic and look at the kind gentleman who saved my life. He has kind eyes and soft hands.

Exceptionally good looking too, with a big warm smile, I'm immediately and overwhelmingly attracted to him. I stare at his lips for a good three seconds before I notice him looking at me with a big smile in his eyes. It's like instant electricity.

Out of nowhere, two complete strangers form a deep connection with just a smile, a few words and a touch.

I suddenly become conscious of myself.

What am I doing? Where am I? What did I come here for?

I notice that he's still holding my hand. He notices that I'm looking at his hand holding mine and immediately pulls his hand away. My brain can't think of anything except to go towards him and kiss him. And it's almost as if he knows it and is more than willing to oblige. He looks at me as if I'm the first woman he's ever seen. I know from his eyes that if he could, he would rip my clothes off right there in the lobby. He knows that I know this. I know that he knows that I know this. Not an extra word spoken and yet so much has been said between us.

I can't take this anymore. I get up.

Within a split second, he gets up too.

We both stare at each other for a good two seconds. I suppose neither of us knew what to say and yet both of us knew what had happened in the last couple of minutes.

An invisible unbreakable unbearable connection had formed between us. I knew right there that this would lead to something much bigger. You don't get these moments in your life so often and yet when they do happen, they change you in ways that you can never anticipate.

Both of us wanted to stay in the moment forever. And yet we knew we couldn't. Both of us wanted to take this connection forward and see where it went.

And yet we knew we had boundaries to respect.

He seems to recover faster. He puts his hand out as if wanting to shake mine...

"Hi, I'm Neil."

"Hi... I'm... I'm Nalini!"

"Are you alright?!"

"Yes... I will be..."

He puts his hand on mine. He's decided to move things

forward and this was an indication that he didn't care about any formal boundaries.

"I think I've fallen in love with you! I think you should know that. Because if you want to take it..."

"I have an interview at Variety today. I'm already late. I'm sorry!"

I walk away towards the elevator because I knew that if I stayed there for another second, I would end up kissing him and who knows what else.

As I reach the elevators, I turn back and look at him. He's nowhere to be seen.

"I'm right here and I'm not going away anywhere."

I turn to my left and find him standing right next to me.

My face goes red as I blush. I think blushing is like an orgasm for the face. It's the finale of everything I feel right now. The elevator door opens with a ding. I hurriedly rush into it before it goes away. He follows me and stands behind me. I just stand there in thrall, amazed at how quickly one incident seemed to have such a huge impression on me.

I thought I had trained my mind to never let anyone, let alone a stranger, a man, ever have any kind of impact on me. I thought that I had good control over my emotions and how I dealt with them. And yet here I was, helplessly, hopelessly, cluelessly falling head over heels in love with this man called Neil.

I clutch my folder tightly against my chest and stare at the elevator door to avoid eye contact with him. For some inexplicable reason he doesn't do anything. He just stands there. I gently let my elbow rub against his clothes. I don't know what's happening to me. He doesn't react. Seconds later, the elevator reaches the 23rd floor. He puts his hand out front and keeps the elevator door open.

"After you..."

I look at him, then look away. I don't know how I'm going to get through the day. He's a cruel man and he loves playing with me. He knows what I'm going through and all he can do is smile. I struggle to snap back into reality.

Variety's office, like the building's lobby, looks very different during the day with the sun streaming in, making it look brighter and bigger, bursting with energy of the people working there.

I look around nervously as I suddenly become aware of my situation.

I'm in the office of the man who destroyed my life and killed my family. I was here less than 48 hours ago, when I stole confidential information from his laptop and am at risk of being recognised and arrested.

I have changed my appearance since the break in and I can only hope that I will not be recognised. I push my thumb nail into my index finger as if wanting to become conscious of all the threats around me.

"See you later!" Says the same dreamy voice as he walks past me.

Fuck!

This is definitely not what I had expected or prepared for. I think I'm in love with this man and want nothing but to make him mine. And yet, I must stick to my goal. I came here to destroy the monster called Shiv Patel and I must stick to my task. Come what may. Focus!

"Please fill out this form and Mr. Patel will see you shortly."

A well-groomed brunette sitting behind the reception desk hands me a clipboard and a pen. I sit on the couch next to the big palm plant by the slanting window.

The view from here is spectacular with the free-flowing Fraser River in the foreground and the snowcapped mountains in the back; the sunlight hitting the tall glass buildings giving them a golden hew. It takes me less than 2 minutes to fill out the form and I hand it back to the receptionist.

"Ms. Shah, please have a seat, you'll be called when your turn comes."

I stand looking out, taking in the beautiful view and

preparing myself to come face to face with the Monster. I brace myself and put every ounce of concentration I have into staying focused and not thinking of Mr. Kind-Eyes-Dreamy-Voice-Neil.

As I'm sitting there my mind wanders. I begin to remember all the things that lead me to this moment, when I'm sitting in the monster's office interviewing to work with his firm. It seemed impossible some years ago and yet, here I was.

I sigh, close my eyes and fold my arms around my chest.

"Please protect me today, I need you both and I wish I could hug you even if it is for a moment." I whisper softly as tears trickle down my eyes.

"I'm pretty sure the air conditioning isn't cranked up that much, I can have it lowered if you're cold."

Same dreamy whisper and again so close to me, I close my eyes, inhale deeply and wipe my tears away discreetly before facing the guy who makes my heart skip a beat every time he comes close to me.

"I'm fine, thank you. Don't you have any work to do?"

I squint as I look at him, trying hard to hide the blush on my cheeks – I don't want him to think of me as someone very desperate. But I feel my heart thumping against my chest, my cheeks burning and butterflies in my stomach as he warmly gazes at me and gives me the cutest smile.

"Ms. Shah, please follow me, you are next."

The elegant brunette in her tight pencil skirt walks ahead holding a folder. He holds my arm, as I'm about to leave, "Coffee after?" He winks playfully and gently lets my hand go.

"Come in and close the door behind you."

I walk into a spacious office with a huge thick wooden desk in the middle, a massive bookcase with hundreds of books stands behind the desk. There is a white couch with bright red cushions on one side of the room sharing space with a mini refrigerator. The walls are adorned with expensive artwork and the big clean windows let the sunlight stream in uninterrupted, making the room look bright and bigger than it looked last evening. Standing in front of me is the guy responsible for turning my whole life upside down. I quietly walk in and close the door behind me.

Mr. Shiv Patel seems to be staring at a sketch on his table. I struggle hard to control my nerves as I wait for him to let me take a seat. He looks up straight into my eyes and stares for what seems like eternity. It's amazing all the things that body language can tell us. I knew in that instant that this man hated me. He stared at me the way a lion would stare at a lamb before attacking it and tearing it into pieces. Maybe he was assessing me as a job candidate. Or maybe not. There was something in his eyes that told me there was much more going on behind those cruel cunning eyes.

What if he'd figured out who I was? Or what if he had found out that I was the intruder in his office the day before yesterday? Is this the last day of my life? All kinds of thoughts raced through my head in the few seconds that we stood there staring at each other. Mr. Shiv Patel finally sits down on his chair. Brace yourself!

Just then the door opens behind me.

I turn back and it's Mr. Kind-Eyes-Dreamy-Voice-Neil again. He quietly pulls a chair and goes and sits next to the Monster. Before I can figure out what is going on...

"Why did the dog bark at you when you came in?"

This wasn't the interview I was expecting. Think.

"I don't know Mr. Patel. Maybe he's just an aggressive dog who doesn't like strangers."

Mr. Patel doesn't say a word. Neil looks at me puzzled and then at Mr. Patel.

"But Bruno isn't known to attack anyone. Our dogs only attack when they suspect something."

I stare back at him. Maybe he could sense the fear in me. Put you game face on girl. I inhaled deeply as I struggled to think of an appropriate answer to his question.

"Have you been to my office before?"

I exhale slowly as I answer in a steely voice.

"No Mr. Patel. This is the first time. Is there a problem?"

Reminding him that he's not behaving politely with me was a good tactic. I pressed on.

"Maybe you've misunderstood who I am. I'm Nalini Shah. I've applied for the job of Interior Designer in your company. I thought I was called in for an interview with you."

"You're more than qualified for the job. We both know that. Which brings me to the question, why are you applying here? You could get a job anywhere. Even in New York."

"I like Vancouver. I'm fond of this place and..." Before I can complete my reply, he cuts in, "Tell me about your background. About your family. Where are you from?"

Neil finally speaks up. "Dad, what's going on? Just let her sit and settle down..."

"How many times have I told you not to bother me when I'm in a meeting?

When will you learn?"

"But dad..."

The sudden revelation that Neil was in fact 'The Neil Patel' - playboy son of Shiv Patel hits me like a ton of bricks.

Carol and I had created a profile of Shiv Patel's playboy son who's been using and dumping girls but this Neil seemed to me nothing like the image that I had in my mind.

Again, not what I was expecting.

When you're an orphan struggling to grow up and manage your affairs entirely on your own without anyone to look after you and support you, you grow up really fast. You become much more inward looking and focused on the few things that really matter to you because you know that there is no one to protect you if things go wrong. I had over the years, learnt to protect myself by anticipating everything that could happen to me and being prepared for it. And yet, today wasn't going my way. At all.

Everything that could go wrong was going wrong.

"Ahem, Ms. Shah, you feeling ok?"

I look up to find Neil looking at me affectionately.

I nod back as I struggle to figure out how to get out on top of this situation.

"You haven't answered my question!" said Shiv Patel his booming voice.

Everything was unravelling right in front of my eyes. I knew that Shiv Patel suspected me. But I didn't know how much he already knew. He definitely thought that I was an imposter but didn't have proof, else he'd get me arrested if not shot.

And this question about my parents and my background also meant that he suspected my fake identity. Was he just fishing or was it more than that? I clear my throat and gather my confidence before responding.

"I ummm, I'm the only child of the most loving parents one can ask for."

I feel a lump in my throat and before I can stop, my eyes well up and before I can stop, a tear rolls down my eye.

"Hey, you okay?" Dreamy voice sounds concerned, I quickly wipe the tear and give him a smile – a sad smile.

"Why did you cry when you spoke about your parents? Do you not live with them?"

The same cold, piercing voice that would send chills down the spine of even the strongest person. Take back control of this conversation. Don't lead him into the truth. Focus, girl!

I look at him, sigh and shake my head.

"Can we not talk about this please. I'm here for a job interview. Not to discuss
family."

He gives me a 'you-really-want-me-to-believe-your-fake-tears?' look and curtly says, "well then why don't we move on, where did you do your schooling from and this time please try not to break down."

I hate this guy! I wish I could kill him right here right now.

If I had a gun, I probably would have. But... Neil was his son. How can the most despicable monster I've ever known have a son as kind as Neil? Neil butts into the conversation. Trying to pacify his father and keep me calm.

"So, Ms. Shah, let's talk about your certifications. Please tell us why you want to work at Variety."

I look at Neil and try to relax as I see him smiling that warm, caring smile that makes me feel fuzzy, like a teenager in love.

"I did my graduation from Emily Karr University and then did my masters at BCIT and now here I am. About why Variety. Because it's the biggest real estate company in Vancouver and working here would get me wide ranging experience along with all the knowledge and skills I need to run my own interior designing firm someday!"

"Hmmm, before we offer you the job, we need to do a background check on you which will involve a police clearance certificate – company policy. Hope you are okay with that?"

As Shiv says these words, I feel like I've been punched in the gut and suddenly feel nauseous. Shiv is like a lion who can smell blood. He's already sensed that I was hiding something. It's like he's turned my entire world upside down in a matter of minutes. What does he know about me? Why is he asking so many probing questions? Has he already figured me out in this first meeting itself? I need to get out of here. I need to make sure both Carol and I are safe. Shiv Patel is a much more dangerous adversary than I'd anticipated.

"You didn't reply. Are you saying that you're not open to us doing a background check on you?"

Beads of sweat form on my forehead and my throat is parched as I try to think of an excuse to get out of this mess. But before I can speak up.

"Miss Shah, do you want this job? Are you ready to get a background check done or are you so ashamed of your background, your upbringing that you'd rather work at a place where they don't care about your background? What is it about your background that is so shameful that you're resisting a background check? What are you trying to hide? Could it be that your parents weren't honest workers at their place of work – come on, help me understand, will you?"

Neil butts in again. Trying to calm the situation down.

"Dad, what's going on? Why are you behaving like this? All she did was apply for a job."

Shiv doesn't reply. Instead he keeps staring at Nalini Shah. She was that child whose parents were dead because of his negligence and over the years he's kept a close watch on her, monitoring which foster homes she was taken to and paid both the Davidsons and that son of a bitch Jack to keep her in control. He had spent thousands of dollars to ensure that that young girl would never be able to cause any trouble for him and yet when he looks at Nalini Shah sitting in front of him now, all he could think of was that young orphan girl.

Neil looks at me and starts talking in his dreamy voice but I can barely hear anything. The Monster, Shiv Patel, just tore apart my confidence and my calmness.

I realise that I'm not as centred as I need to be, to ace this situation. I'm barely able to control my nausea. I gather up all my courage and manage to speak up.

I look directly into Shiv Patel's eyes.

"I don't want this job. Not because I care about some background check that you want to do. But because of your hostile and humiliating attitude. Ever since I've come to your office, you've been nothing but rude and obnoxious with me. I will not accept that. That is no way to behave with a woman... especially not someone like me who can add so much value to your organization. I've struggled my whole life to excel at what I do and if you'd cared to look at my certifications, you would have known that I got a scholarship for my Masters. That doesn't happen so easily. So please keep this job. Hire someone else who will accept your insulting, condescending, patriarchal behaviour."

I dig my nails into my palms as I make a fist.

Shiv Patel tore apart the persona I had created with years of pain staking effort. In that moment, I could have killed him because that's how desperate I was to get my revenge.

Instead I just get up, collect my folder and storm out of Variety's office crying in anger, oblivious of the people around me

Neil gets up to come after me to try and pacify me but Shiv Patel shouts angrily at him. "Let her go. We don't need her."

"Why Dad? What did she do that you went all ballistic on her?"

"There is something wrong with this girl. She's not who she appears to be."

"There you go again. Always paranoid and suspicious of everyone."

"It's only the paranoid who survive Neil. I didn't build a multi-million-dollar company without knowing my way around people. And I'm telling you. This girl is no good. She's not straightforward. We don't want her. Stay away from her."

Neil screams out in frustration, "Fuck! You're impossible Dad!"

He rushes out of the office.

A lot of people notice me crying as I stumble my way out of the Variety building.

Neil catches up with me and grabs my arm just as I am about to exit out of the main door. "Please Miss Shah, just give me a chance to explain. My dad is not a bad guy at heart – he's just a bit moody and I will talk to him, I promise."

He wipes off the tears flowing down my cheeks.

"I don't want this job Mr. Neil Patel. I'm sorry."

"Don't be so formal with me please. Just give me a chance and I promise I'll get you this job. This is my company as much as it is his. And he will listen to me."

"Even if you do manage to get me the job, why should I accept it? I can't deal with your father."

"You won't have to. You'll have to report to me. Not my father. I'll keep him out of your way. I promise."

I look away not wanting to commit. I need him to try harder and commit himself to my cause...

"I've never felt this way about anyone ever before. I can't let you go."

"I'm not sure if..."

"Promise me that you'll accept this job if I manage to convince my dad. Please?!"

"I'll think about it."

I turn around and walk away leaving him heartbroken.

Unknown to the both of us, Shiv Patel is watching us via the surveillance camera feed that comes directly into his laptop. His head of security is standing in front of him hoping not to get yelled at.

"I showed a photo of this Nalini Shah to the security guard from that night. But he's not sure if it's the same girl."

Shiv shakes his head then looks at the both of us on his laptop screen.

"There goes the bloody fool. Wagging his tail like a dog in front of a girl he knows nothing about. Why can't he grow up into a man? Why does he have to be such a lovelorn puppy?"

The head of security knows that it's a rhetorical comment and wasn't really a question he was expected to answer. He keeps quiet.

Shiv keeps looking at Neil pleading and imploring Nalini to give him a chance and shouts.

"Stupid boy!"

Shiv watches Nalini leave the building complex. The Head of Security takes this as a cue and excuses himself. Shiv then sits back in his chair, hands on his head and eyes closed – hoping all this is just a dream. Then abruptly picks up his coat and leaves the office.

ADRIAN RAY IS WALKING at a brisk pace. He had to make sure that no one was following him. Shiv was the one person in all of

Canada that he didn't want to disappoint in any way. His life in Canada depended on keeping Shiv happy and he was paid very well for his services. He's now on a narrow lane behind a greasy Asian restaurant that was always empty.

Once he was absolutely confident that the street was empty and there were no surveillance cameras around... he takes out his phone and sends his location pin.

Within a few minutes, Shiv's car appears. Adrian looks around one last time, then opens the door and sits in the car.

Shiv looks at Adrian – a Canadian Asian 35-year-old guy who was a wanted criminal in South East Asia. Shiv trusted him completely because he could get Adrian arrested and deported any time he wanted. Adrian knew this and so was always deferential towards Shiv.

"You keep getting thinner every year."

Adrian bows to his biggest client and smiles.

Shiv knows from years of experience that Adrian wasn't the kind who liked to talk a lot, so he comes to the point very quickly.

"I interviewed a young twenty something girl today and this is her resume. I have a strong feeling that she is the same kid from that accident."

Adrian looks at Shiv surprised. Shiv nods.

"Yes. We need to find out everything about this girl. So, do a thorough job on this one and do it as quickly as possible."

He hands over another, smaller, bulkier envelope, "this is the first half of the payment, rest once the job is done."

Without saying another word, Adrian leaves the car.

As the car quietly moves out of the shady dark neighbourhood, a grim looking Shiv stares at the road pensively.

Chapter Four

Nalini tosses unconsciously in her bed, beads of sweat trickling down her forehead. She throws the comforter on the ground and rolls on her stomach groaning loudly.

"In just a few hours, we will be in a new place, ready to start a new life."

I've never seen dad so excited, he can't stop looking out of the small window desperately waiting for our plane to land on the mystical, magical land of opportunities: Canada.

Mum and Dad decided to move to another country so that they can give me a better life and it wasn't easy for them as both had to quit their well-paying jobs and a comfortable life in India. We land at the YVR international airport and begin our life afresh in a new country that we now call home. Dad smiles and ushers mum and me out of the airport as we head out into our new lives.

Mum and Dad take turns to go to work so that I am not alone in our basement home. Mum works at Best Buy and does a morning shift, while Dad does a night shift working for a security company.

"So, who's ready to spend the day on the beach, it's Funday Sunday; come on people, wake up..."

Dad is excited and has been planning this small getaway for a couple of weeks now. I hear Mum toiling away in the kitchen making her famous egg and cheese sandwiches and packing a nice picnic basket. Being the only child has a lot of advantages; one of them being pampered endlessly.

Mum and Dad always go out of their way to fulfil my wishes and going for a picnic is one of them. We pack a nice basket, a bag with a change of clothes for me along with a few toys and head out to downtown Vancouver.

It's a nice sunny day, the beach is filled with people sun bathing and luckily, we find a nice shady spot. As always Mum fusses over me and slops what seems like a gallon of sunscreen on my face, legs and arms as I continue to whine and protest.

"Let's go sweetheart, the water awaits us."

Dad is very dramatic and loves to bring dialogues into his conversations.

Mum and I exchange glances, roll our eyes and I drag dad into the Pacific Ocean.

Dad and I swim and play in the water for a couple hours till I get hungry. I drag him out towards Mum who is sitting with a towel ready to wipe me down and change me into clean dry clothes. We have a nice lunch of egg and cheese sandwiches along with chips and Coca Cola, followed by a nice chocolate ice cream cone and before I know, it's time for us to go home.

I am very tired but ecstatic, after a very long time we've had a nice time together as a family. Dad puts me to bed, he drops a kiss on my forehead and turns off the bedside lamp.

"Daddy, thank you. I love you too." I kiss his cheek and laugh as he playfully nuzzles against my neck and puts me back on the bed.

"It's my happy birthday... Mum, Dad... it's my 10th birrrrthday!"

I'm jumping on the bed and screaming with joy.

"Nisha, stop jumping on the bed, get down and go take a shower."

Mum lifts me and carries me to the washroom as I continue to sing happy birthday to me.

We've been in Canada for almost a year now and we've bought our own apartment and a second-hand car which both Mum and Dad drive, while I sit in the back seat. Dad takes me to the mall to buy me a new dress that makes me look like a princess. I love it! I love both my parents so much. I can't imagine my life without them. He smiles and tells me how much he loves me and that he will do anything to see me happy and put a smile on my face.

"Does my little princess want to have a cone of ice cream?"

He lifts me up and puts me on his shoulders as we head towards Purdy's ice cream store in the mall; the world looks so nice from up here. I feel like I'm on the top of the mountain and have a clear view of the world below. I get my favourite ice cream flavour and I happily eat it.

"Nisha, you need to stand still, let me braid your hair properly."

Mum is dressing me up for my birthday treat and I'm impatient as ever. She hugs and kisses me as I pull away wanting to rush to the party. Dad lifts me up and swirls me around as I laugh uncontrollably while Mum goes to get dressed.

I am happy as Mum and Dad are taking me to a restaurant for dinner to celebrate my birthday and have showered me with so many gifts.

"Mommy, hurry up, we will get late."

It is getting harder for me to contain my excitement and I keep running in and out of the apartment, calling the elevator and yelling.

After Mum's 45 minute make up routine, my constant yelling and running, we are finally on our way to the restaurant. We pull into the driveway of my favourite restaurant Chucky Cheese and I squeal with joy unable to contain my happiness. Mum and Dad exchange glances and smile at each other.

"Now hold still and let me tie this properly, no peaking."

Mum has tied a scarf around my eyes and both Mum and Dad hold my hands as they walk me into the restaurant. "Surprise! Happy Birthday Nisha..."

After we've entered the restaurant, my Mum suddenly takes off the scarf and I'm overwhelmed to see all my friends and everyone I know inside the restaurant. I cry tears of joy as I'd never expected such a big surprise. I hug Mum and Dad as I look around and take in everything.

The whole place is decked up; there are red, blue, gold and silver balloons along with satin ribbons and glitter. I feel so happy and quietly thank God for giving me the parents I have. They shower me with so much love that I feel blessed.

My friends and I thoroughly enjoy the party and in no time we're all high on sugar from all the candy floss, juices and general excitement. We run around aimlessly, chasing each other, screaming with joy; completely unmindful of the world around us.

Finally, a huge velvet cake arrives with my face on it the magical words: HAPPY BIRTHDAY NISHA written on it!

Like bees attracted to honey, all the children swamp around the cake hoping to get the best view and piece. I actually feel like a Princess and bask in the attention being given to me, after all it is my day and I want to soak every minute of it. As I blow the candles, Dad pops a balloon over my head releasing all the confetti it held. Mum and Dad feed me a piece of the cake while the photographer takes our pictures. This is followed by numerous people coming and feeding me pieces of the cake and getting their photos taken with me. Today, I'm no less than a movie star.

IT IS ALMOST 10 pm and we have started wrapping up. I hand out the return gifts to my friends, who in turn thank me for a wonderful party before leaving.

We drive out of the parking lot and the roads are full of water. The radio host cautions people to drive carefully in these extreme conditions and Dad slows down the car and moves to the right lane. I keep drifting in and out of sleep as the streetlights bother me from time to time.

SUDDENLY THERE IS a huge bang and I wake up to our car spinning out of control before crashing into an electric pole nearby.

"Mommy, daddy, I'm scared."

I struggle to unbuckle my seat belt but it is stuck and Mum and Dad are also not moving. I am cold, scared and cry helplessly dazed by the suddenness of what has happened.

"Mommy wake up, please wake up, I'm scared."

A FEW MINUTES later the whole place is filled with fire trucks, ambulances and police cars, blocking the intersection and people in uniforms running around trying to break open our car doors.

The whole street is covered with an oil spill from our car and another car standing on the opposite side of the road. The pouring rain is making it difficult for everyone to do their jobs properly.

"It's ok honey, we'll get you out of here in no time."

A kind fire fighter cuts open the back door of our car, cuts the seat belt and pulls me out of the, now burning car and rushes me to an ambulance. The paramedics act swiftly and cover me with warm blankets and clean me with warm wipes.

"Where are my Mum and Dad?"

I'm shivering and look around trying to find them but all I see are two piles covered with tarp and numerous people taking pictures.

A tall well-built bearded guy staggers towards me but is stopped by a young cop who ties his hands and takes him away. He looks back as he walks away and smirks at me which makes me scared.

"Hey sweetheart, we are going to take you to the hospital to get checked up by a doctor, okay."

I nod unwillingly and wipe the constantly flowing tears with the back of my hand as I let out a big yawn. I am tired and can barely keep my eyes open.

THE NEXT THING I know is that I'm being driven away from the accident site; I cry as I see the two tarp piles become smaller and finally disappearing into the darkness.

"Hi Nisha, I am Dr. Roy Scott and I am here to make sure that you are comfortable and warm."

An elderly kind faced man smiles at me as he puts the stethoscope on my chest to listen to my heartbeat. After a couple of more tests he gently puts his hand on my head, gives me a warm smile and drops a kiss on my forehead the same way as Dad did when he tucks me in.

"Goodnight sweetheart, you look fine to me. You sleep well and I'll check on you tomorrow morning."

I wake up screaming for Mum and Dad.

"It's ok sweetie, shhh... It's ok try to sleep. You've had a bad dream, it's ok."

I wrap my arms around a young nurse who rocks me to sleep while another checks my temperature and gives me a pill to calm me down.

"GOOD MORNING NISHA. How are you feeling today?" Dr. Roy stands next to my bed holding my wrist to check my pulse.

"When will I meet my parents? I miss them, are they okay?" Tears roll down my eyes as I look at him, hoping he will take me to my parents and I will finally be with them. Dr. Roy kisses my forehead, gives me a tight hug and a smile that is filled with sadness. I have lost track of time and all I can think of are my parents. I wish someone would tell me how they are, where are they and when will I be with them. I feel lost and lonely without them.

A couple of hours later, a nurse takes me to meet Dr. Carla Brown, a young doctor with the sweetest voice who sits in front of me, smiling warmly.

"Hi Nisha, I'm Dr. Carla Brown. I'm here to become your friend and get to know you, so today, we will spend some time together and you are free to ask me anything you want. Will you be my friend?"

I look at her beaming at me and I am unable to understand why am I meeting doctors and not Mum and Dad.

I sit quietly sit on a chair and nod "Yes".

"Now Nisha, I have been told that you're wanting to meet your Mum and Dad and also that you miss them, am I right?"

I nod without looking up.

"Do you remember what happened last night when you were coming home?"

I nod again.

"Oh honey, I am really sorry to tell you this but you and your parents were involved in a very serious accident last night and your Mommy and Daddy have passed away."

I burst into tears and am unable to cope with this reality. She hugs me and I think she is crying.

"Love, your Mommy and Daddy are dead and they cannot come back ever, I'm so sorry."

I feel like I've been punched hard and cannot feel my legs.

The room suddenly starts spinning and everything becomes black.

. . .

I WAKE up to a room full of nurses, Dr. Roy and Dr. Carla talking in low tones while occasionally glancing at me. Both the doctors come and stand on each side of my bed.

"Hey princess, how are you now?"

I look up at Dr. Roy beaming at me and softly whisper.

"Are my Mommy and Daddy dead?"

Dr. Roy perches on the edge of the bed, takes me in his arms and hugs me, "I am so sorry sweetheart. I wish I could wave a magic wand and rewind the time to get your Mommy and Daddy back, but we can definitely get you a new Mommy and Daddy who will love you equally and provide you with a happy safe home."

I feel a lump in my throat, I am shivering and I snuggle closer to that kind gentleman, who's been like a father figure since I got to the hospital.

I cry for an hour or so, I don't remember the exact time. Dr. Roy continues to hold me and console me but the thought of never seeing my parents again terrifies me.

I AM INTRODUCED TO A TALL, slim lady wearing a business suit carrying a black handbag and a folder. She holds out her hand for me to shake it as if she's meeting an adult and not a 10-year-old who's just lost both her parents.

I hide behind Dr. Carla.

"Hi Nisha, I am Ms. Jill Shaw, I am going to help you get adopted so that you get a family soon."

I cling to Dr. Carla, who picks me up and wipes off my tears for the umpteenth time. "What is it honey? This nice lady will find a new Mommy and Daddy for you and a loving home."

I cringe at the thought and scream, "I DON'T want another Mommy and Daddy, I want MY Mum and Dad and I DON'T like her."

I get down and run away to be alone. After a lot of

comforting and consoling, I am finally sent to family services with Ms. Shaw to be put up for adoption or sent to a foster home.

"Cindy, this is Nisha Shah, she just lost her parents in a car crash and will be here till we find a family for her. Please show her room and make sure she feels comfortable here."

JILL instructs a young receptionist at Family Services, who looks bored and gives me a look that sends shivers down my spine.

The room she takes me to is small with a spring bed on one side, a small study table and chair on the other, along with a chest of drawer for my clothes and a stand for my shoes.

"So, this is your room and the bathroom is right outside on the left. Make yourself comfortable and hope you sleep well, Goodnight." Cindy gives me a bottle of water, a comforter and a set of night wear and a pair of slippers before leaving me alone in a cold, semi dark room.

I wake up sweating and crying, calling out to Mum and Dad, I'm so terrified that I wet the bed; the room is dark and the cold wet bed is making me shiver.

"I miss you both, I'm so scared. Mommy, Daddy, please come back."

I finally curl up and cry myself to sleep, unsure what tomorrow will bring and feeling vulnerable.

"GOOD MORNING, Nisha. Did you sleep well? Get dressed, we have someone coming to meet you today and hopefully, you will get a family soon."

In less than an hour, I am dressed in a new set of clothes and taken to the foster home of Mr. and Mrs. Davidson, a middle-aged white couple who seem kind and caring. They introduce me to their two children, a girl and a boy. Both children don't like that I am moving in with them and make it very clear.

While Jill and the Davidsons talk, I sit like a porcelain doll hoping that they don't take me in. I don't like it here especially with both the kids standing in the hallway making faces and poking fun at me.

"So, Nisha, this is going to be your new home. Be nice and stay out of trouble, I'll come to check in on you soon." Jill leaves without giving me a hug and I feel so lonely and out of place.

Mrs. Davidson notices her children making faces at me. She sits her two children down next to me and tells them to behave themselves.

Both Sally and John smirk at me and leave.

"Don't worry about these two, they will come around. This is our first time having a foster child live with us and they are not used to it. Come, I'll show you your room, get you settled just in time for dinner."

I quietly follow Mrs. Davidson or Debra into a nice room with a comfy bed in the middle with a few toys lined on it, a big window with lace curtains, a small dresser and chest of drawers, bean bags to sit on and a study desk with a small chair in one corner.

"Leave your bags here, let's go have dinner; then you can come, have a shower and sleep."

I envy their family dinnertime and it makes me miss Mum and Dad even more. They are a close-knit family and I am constantly made to feel like an outsider. I excuse myself and go into my room. Life is not what it used to be and I am unable to accept this change.

The next day onwards Debra makes me do house work all the time and yells at me if I get a little late for mealtime. Her husband Garry keeps his distance from me.

A FEW DAYS LATER, I see the same tall, well built, bearded man from the accident night meet Garry outside our home and say something to him. He gives him an envelope and leaves in his big flashy car.

The next day onwards, I find Garry paying a lot more attention to me. He keeps asking me to get something or the other for him. I don't understand this constant attention I'm getting from him but I keep doing everything he asks me to.

"SALLY, John and I are going to the mall, make sure the house is dusted and clean. Garry is at home, if you need anything."

I see them leave and wish I too could go with them, but there are different rules for me. I start loading the dishwasher when Garry calls out to me, "Nisha, get me a glass of water and make it fast."

I fill a glass of water and carry it to his room carefully.

"Come in and close the door behind you," Garry calls out as I knock on the door.

I am horrified as I step into his room; the curtains are drawn, the lights dimmed and Garry is sitting on his bed, completely naked. I quiver as I put the glass on the side table and try to rush out of the room, but he catches me and pulls me closer to him.

"Mr. Davidson, please, I don't like it, you're like my father, please let me go."

I wriggle to get out of his grip but he is strong and I am unable to and plead one more time as he tries to kiss me and undress me.

"You'll like it, come on, I know you also want it."

He forces me to touch his penis which is hard and gross and as he tries to fondle me, I push him, run out of his room and into mine and lock it up till Debra, Sally and John come back.

"She's been behaving weirdly since morning. I asked her to get me a glass of water and she just was all over me, trying to kiss me and touch me." I hear Garry telling Debra even before I can go and talk to her.

. . .

"Nisha, open the damn door, you slut. How dare you? I leave you for one hour and you try to hit on my husband. Come out and let me show you your place, open the damn door." She continues to bang the door till I open it and look her in the eye.

"If you even think of touching me, I will tell Jill how you treat me. I will tell her that I don't want to live here anymore and that will stop the government funding you get for keeping me here. I know it and it was your husband who was sitting naked and tried to make me touch his thing. So, you decide what you want as it is Jill's quarterly visit tomorrow."

I slam the door on her face and lie on the bed face down crying.

I cry myself to sleep that night. I just cannot believe that my life would get ruined so fast. I sleep hungry, as I'm not called for dinner and I can hear the family talking and laughing. I wake up the next morning with nausea and a splitting headache.

"Nisha, Jill is here, come down, we have a lot to talk about."

I come down and see Debra and Garry fill Jill in about my behaviour and tantrums; she does not look happy and keeps noting down everything she's being told. Jill invites me to go out with her and spend some time together so we end up at a McDonalds where I order a happy meal and Jill orders a coffee.

"So, tell me, and don't leave out any details, what happened?"

I'm initially hesitant to tell her everything but Jill eventually coaxes everything out of me. She is really horrified at what has happened and tells me to go back with her so that we can pick up all my stuff and leave permanently.

It's been a week since I moved out of the Davidson's home and Jill told me that they will never get to foster another child and Garry has been charged with child molestation. Within a week, I'm taken to meet another family.

❄

A YOUNG 40-YEAR-OLD man Jack who lives with a foster child called Emma and his wife Rhonda. He says all the right things and seems to be concerned about my abuse in the previous foster home so I accept being moved into his house.

I FINALLY MEET Emma - a young blond girl, my age, who comes down and sits across from me looking me straight in the eye, "so you're the new girl. Welcome, I hope you like it here; come, let me show you our room." She gives me the sweetest smile, takes my hand and leads me upstairs.

"You take good care of her Emma." Jack calls out from behind. Emma stops, turns around and with a smirk on her face says, "Jack, you don't need to tell me what to do." She looks at me and scoffs, "Just ignore him, he's not important."

We enter a nice room with two beds with a middle table in between, baby pink walls, lace curtains, a couple of study desks and a walk-in closet. The iron rod beds have spring mattress with satin sheets and feather pillows along with soft plush comforters. "Come on in, feel at home. The right-side bed is mine, so that leaves you with the left side. You can place your bag in the closet and let me take you around the house."

I HAVE STARTED LIKING this Emma girl, she is so cool and chilled out; I already feel comfortable with her and at home. I look around the room while she sits on her bed and quietly observes me, "It's nice to have you here, I've always wanted a friend and I hope that we can become best friends." I nod and smile as I sit on my bed, trying to avoid any eye contact with her.

We finish dinner, I help Emma wash dishes and clear the table when Jack calls out, "Emma, please send Nisha upstairs with my beer and ask her to hurry up."

We exchange looks and Emma sighs loudly, "not again and not on her first night here."

I give her a confused look. Emma looks at me concerned, "Just try and not go into the room."

THE ROOM UPSTAIRS is dark with a dimly lit floor lamp on one corner, a king size bed in the middle and a huge television mounted on the wall across from the bed.

It is larger than our room with an attached-on suite bathroom and a door that leads to the patio. The door is open but I still knock and stand waiting for Jack to respond. Another knock and I cautiously walk in holding the beer mug tightly as if scared I will drop it and get into trouble for spilling the beer on the carpet.

Emma suddenly comes in and whispers to me to put the glass on the side table and run out. "Well, now did I ask you to come with her?"

We scream and turn around to find Jack standing in the doorway blocking our exit of his room. "Jack, you cannot do this, we have to go." Emma takes my hand and tries to walk out but is stopped by Jack who starts walking towards us, smiling with his head tilted, "now, now, let's not make a big deal out of it instead let's make it a night to remember."

It is a night of horror for both of us as he closes the door, sits and starts drinking while we huddle together in a corner hoping that he would pass out.

An hour later, he finally gets ups, staggers into the washroom to pee, "this is our chance, let's go, he won't notice and won't remember anything in the morning." Emma whispers to me as she takes my hand and runs towards the door.

"Where on this earth do you think you are going? Get back in here, now!"

We slowly turn around and are horrified to see him standing naked, he raises his eyebrows and says to Emma, "Now do I need to tell you what to do, get down here. You have to pay to live here and this is how you pay."

Emma starts to walk up to him but I keep holding her hand

tightly and pull her back. He looks at me and chuckles, "so now you will stand up for her, why don't you come and take a taste of the best." He points towards his penis hanging between his legs and asks me to come and suck it.

"Don't!" Emma yells at me. "There is no need for you to do this!"

"Do it, or I starve the both of you!" Jack says in a menacing voice. "Yes! Both of you!"

Emma, tries to stop me but I slowly go and sit on my knees, take his hanging penis in my mouth and start moving my head back and forth. After a couple of minutes, he suddenly pushes me away and runs into the washroom, Emma and I leave the room and I brush my teeth vigorously hoping to undo what I was forced to do.

AFTER FORTY-FIVE MINUTES of being in the washroom, I finally muster the courage to come out and face Emma hoping that she would not judge me. Instead to my surprise, she hugs me till I break down and cry my heart out.

Emma asks me to complain to Jill and get the hell out of this house. She cries as she tells me that this is how it was for her and how it's always going to be. I'm surprised at how matter-of-fact she is about her life.

I ask her why she hasn't complained and she tells me that she's an abandoned child. That her parents didn't want her and her experience in successive foster homes had made her feel rejected everywhere she went. That she had made peace with all the things she needed to do to survive. She tells me that there were good foster homes for girls who got lucky and they lived good lives. Seeing her open up to me and talk about her life breaks my heart. I decide not to complain to Jill about anything and instead be with Emma since she's the only friend I had left in the whole wide world. We sit on the bed holding each other, two ten-year-olds, being each other's strength, finding solace in each other's company.

"We'll be fine, we will come out of this stronger, we got each other." Emma keeps repeating this while rocking me back and forth, we finally curl up and fall asleep together in her bed holding each other and hugging each other.

On that night and completely unexpectedly ten-year-old-me had grown up into an adult and understood was life was all about for an orphan girl.

I knew what to expect from life but something in me kept telling me to fight back.

Little did I know, this was just the beginning, the worst was yet to come.

"Get the fuck out of bed!"

We wake up to Jack towering over us. He suddenly yanks the comforter off us and drags us out of bed.

"I want you both lazy asses down in 15 minutes, I don't have all day to cook for you and feed you. Fifteen minutes and if I don't see either of you at the breakfast table, no food for you."

He storms out leaving us cursing under our breadth.

"Come on, we cannot miss breakfast." Emma jumps out of bed and heads straight to the washroom to pee and brush her teeth.

I reluctantly follow, as I want to catch up on my sleep. After a breakfast of burnt toasts, half boiled eggs and simple warm milk, we are told to clean up and do other chores around the house while Jack sits on the porch smoking a cigarette and having beer.

"What about school? When will we go to school?" I ask him and all I get is a glare and a smirk. Emma tells me that she goes to school only when her case worker comes for a visit and it would be the same for me too and that we should both study at home.

Once again, I muster all the courage I have and walk up to Jack, "Jack, when will we go to school? Can you drop us please?" He smiles and says, "you want to go to school, why don't you go get dressed and I will take you both to school."

Shrieking with joy, both of us run up, shower and get dressed only to get beaten up. My face is red and my ear throbbing from the slap that he gave when we came down with our bags, ready to go.

Emma's hair was pulled and she was kicked in the stomach, "you've been here long enough to know what the rules are and yet instead of teaching her, you join her, you little slut."

He spits on her as she lies curled up on the floor whining in pain. I wait for him to go out, run up to her, help her get up and take her to our room.

"I wish we could run away someday, I hope he gets arrested and dies a horrible death."

Tears roll down her eyes as she hugs herself to ease the pain; it is my time to console her. A couple of hours later, Jack comes in with a few painkillers and sits on the bed opposite Emma.

"How many times have I told you not to anger me? What will you do in school? I've given you all the books and course material. All you have to do is study, which you can do from home. So why insist on going out, when you have everything here?"

Neither of us say anything to him.

"Good. I will give you both lunch in a couple hours."

As soon as he leaves Emma throws the pills away in a fit of rage. The next day onwards, we decide to try and make the best of our situation.

WE FOCUS on studying together despite the repeated interruptions. Just when we somehow manage to take things in our stride and meeting Jack's needs, his wife Rhonda makes an appearance. We are summoned downstairs to meet her.

While walking downstairs, Emma tries to warn me. "Just keep quiet. She's worse than him."

Rhonda is a skinny brunette wearing skin hugging jeans and a tight revealing blouse that shows more than what needs to be seen. She leans on the kitchen island while staring at me...

"So, this is the little devil, our second daughter. Come here, let me see you closely."

She lights a cigarette and blows the smoke on my face making me cough uncontrollably.

"So, you are Nisha!" She walks around me as if scanning every inch of my body, making me uncomfortable. She pulls up a bar stool and sits across from me, gestures to me to come close as she takes another quick smoke before putting out her cigarette.

"Do you know who I am?"

I shake my head fearing that she may hit me for not knowing instead she pulls me closer and looks me in the eye.

"I will tell you this once. I am Jack's wife, I am the owner of this place and I am the one who decides everything here, my name is Rhonda. You need anything, you first ask me, is that clear?"

I once again nod my head nervously wishing that I don't piss her off. Jack comes and stands behind her whispering something in her ear and kissing the back of her neck while fondling her breasts. She gestures to us to go play in the backyard as both of them go up into their room for a good couple of hours.

"She is the one, we need to look out for. She is evil and very mean." Emma tells me as we take turns on the swing.

Dinner time is quiet, with them making out in front of us and we trying to finish our meal as fast as we can. Rhonda suddenly gets up and announces that she is retiring for the day and asks both Emma and me to clear the dinner table before we head back to our room.

"I don't want to see any dishes in the sink and nothing out on the table." Jack, like a puppy dog, follows her as she walks away with an air of indifference.

WE UNDERSTAND the hierarchy in the house and do everything that Rhonda asks us to do. We understand that our lives were built around deception. To avoid being beaten up, we pretend to Jack that we're happy with the way things were and do everything we can to prevent him from getting angry. We lie to him and flatter him into letting us have some time to study. We never tell him the truth about what we're thinking or feeling. This helps us maintain some sanity in our lives.

We eventually end up doing all the work there is to be done just so that we can avoid the violence and pain that are threatened if we don't oblige.

The only thing that keeps us going ahead is that we are studying and have a dream to someday be in control of our lives. It's a dream that Emma and I both share and we swear to always be there for each other throughout our lives.

THEN ONE DAY, the same tall, well built, bearded man makes an appearance. He parks the car at a distance from the house and Jack goes to meet him.

Emma and I both peek out of our room window and look at him. I curiously ask Emma who this man. Emma takes out a bundle of newspapers clippings of the night of the accident and shows it to me. Emma points out the man in the photograph on the night of the accident and then looks at the man standing next to his car.

"That man is called Shiv Patel. He's a real estate millionaire."

Memories of the accident come rushing back to me. For a moment I'm numb as I've never been able to cope with the sudden loss of my parents. Then suddenly everything becomes crystal clear. I remember this man from the night of the accident.

He was the one with the grin on his face, as if he was enjoying seeing me in pain and didn't care. Suddenly it all makes sense to me. It's this man who paid my foster parents to make my life miserable. I had seen him with the Davidsons and now I'm seeing him with Jack. Jack takes a stuffed envelope from him and hides it in his pocket. It doesn't take us much time to figure out what must have happened.

"I'm going to kill this bastard! I'm going to destroy his life!"

Emma tries to calm me down but the rage within me just keeps rising.

"He's the one who killed my parents and condemned me to this shit hole for the rest of my life! I will kill him, even if I have to die for it!"

Emma is taken aback at the intensity of my anger. We don't speak about this again in the house. Emma thinks it is best to also not bring up the topic with Jack or Rhonda.

Days pass into weeks and months slip by.

The endless abuse at the hands of Jack and Rhonda continues unabated, year after year. Even when Jill comes to check on me, I know that I cannot tell her anything because even if I do manage to leave this house, Emma will face the brunt of the abuse and I couldn't do that to the only person I care about. So, we keep our heads down, study hard and try to learn everything we can about a whole lot of subjects that interest us. I help Emma with everything she wants to do and she in turn helps me with all my stuff. We become an unbreakable team.

We learn and understand the value of money and how to earn it. We spend all the time learning and understanding how to make money.

We please Jack and Rhonda and cater to their every whim. Over time, they learn to treat us a little bit better. From the age of fourteen onwards, we learn to flatter them into letting us do the things we want.

Emma and I tell them to get themselves two stock trading accounts that we would manage for them and get them to agree on splitting the profits half way. We use our knowledge of stock trading and trade in the names of Jack and Rhonda from their trading accounts.

Over the next two years, with our share of the profits we get ourselves laptops, phones and books. We learn as much as we can about the world outside this hell hole. Emma learns to be a software programmer and hacker while I learn a wide variety of soft skills, entrepreneurship and management.

Each day we strengthen our unspoken dream, that one day we will leave these abusive parasites and go out into the big bad world.

YEARS PASS by and we're not poor and helpless any more. From two broke ten-year-old-orphaned-abused kids, we become two educated-bright-seventeen-years-old tough-as-nails young women who are worth a hundred-thousand-dollars each and have knowledge about a wide variety of subjects.

We build contacts and connections everywhere using the phone, the internet and the profits we've made with trading in stocks, derivatives and cryptocurrencies.

We know a wide variety of people who can help us do almost anything we want if we paid them the right amount. We've also made enough money to live well for two years without earning anything.

We keep all our money in cash and leave no trace of our actual identities anywhere as we use Jack and Rhonda's identities for everything.

Then one day we realise that we had put together everything it takes to achieve our goals for the next five years. It is time to execute our plan.

IT IS time to leave this miserable life behind us forever.

We wait for the right opportunity until one day we find out

that Jack and Rhonda trust us enough to leave us alone in the house for a few days. We both know that this was the chance we were waiting for.

It's 10 pm and both Emma and I sit on the rooftop on a warm summer night watching the sun go down. The sky turns dark blue with stars spread across like diamonds and a full moon, the size of a beach ball.

I wrap a throw around both of us and take a deep breath as I look into the darkness.

The fragrance of summer flowers looms in the cool air helping me relax and unwind.

We sit in silence and absorb the quiet of the surroundings mixed with an occasional hoot of the barn owl and the clicking sounds of the crickets.

"ONCE THEY'RE GONE, we will pack whatever we can in our backpacks and leave. I've booked a cheap motel in town for a few nights, that should give us time to plan further, but before we go, we have to change the way we look. Cops looking for us is the last thing I want."

I speak softly but firmly, as this will be our one and only chance to get away from Jack and Rhonda.

"Let's go and get some sleep, tomorrow's going to be a long day and who knows when we may get some proper sleep."

She holds out her hand and pulls me up, together we crawl back into our room from the window.

THE NEXT DAY RHONDA, as usual, is going around packing her stuff while barking orders at us and threatening us with dire consequences if we did anything that displeased her. Emma and I exchange glances and roll our eyes; this is not the first time but this surely will be the last. We help her so that they leave soon and we can run away before they even realise.

"Would you like to carry some sandwiches for the road, Rhonda?"

I try to sound as casual as I can. She smiles, something that is very rare – especially with us, and nods her head.

Emma stares at me in disbelief, "what is wrong with you Nisha?" she whispers in anger.

"Calm down, I know what I am doing. You go and start packing our stuff, just lock the room, turn on the shower as if you're in the washroom and I'll manage the rest. Go on, we don't have time"

I nudge her sharply and start making sandwiches.

AN HOUR LATER, Jack and Rhonda leave for the weekend and both Emma and I are left alone in the house. We wait for about ten minutes to ensure that they will not return and then, lock all doors and start collecting stuff to take with us. Rhonda's jewellery, cash from their bedside tables, Jack's expensive watches and some expensive antique artefacts.

"Hurry up our ride out of town will be waiting for us near the bus stand. It'll take us 15 minutes to reach the bus stand and that too if we walk fast or run."

Emma rushes between the rooms holding as much as she could in her arms, we are racing against time.

WITH A BACKPACK each on our shoulders, we are ready to leave and don't even look back. I open the front door and stop in my tracks and gasp loudly; a look of horror on my face. My heart starts beating loudly against my chest – standing in front of us, is our abusive foster father Jack.

"Well, where are we going? You should have told us you wanted to go on a trip, we wouldn't have refused."

He walks up to us forcing us to move back, Emma holds my

hand, as I'm about to make a fist to punch him. He continues to walk and starts taking off his jacket along with his shoes.

"Does Rhonda know you've come here? If you try to touch us, I promise, you will regret it for the rest of your sorry life."

He chuckles and smirks as he continues to walk towards us and suddenly pounces on me and pushes me to the ground. He barks in a voice that sends shivers down my spine as he slaps and punches me.

"You're one feisty bitch and I know how to get you in control."

He pins me down, tears of my shirt and starts to unzip my pants and pulls them down.

"You fucking bitch, I'll show you what it is to go against me. You want to run away from me? I'll make sure you never walk again."

He thrusts his hand inside me and I scream in pain while kicking my legs, but he overpowers me. Suddenly, Emma punches him in the face and he falls on the side.

"You think you control us – you are so wrong. We'll tell you who's the boss here."

I push him off me, pull up my jeans and kick him hard in the stomach. He gets up and punches Emma in the stomach making her crouch and fall on the ground whining in pain.

"That'll teach you not to mess with me, you fucking bitch."

He spits on her, kicks her and looks at me with rage in his eyes, "you bloody bitch, I'll show you your place but first let me deal with this piece of shit."

He bends down and pulls her up by pulling her hair and clenching his teeth he says, "Now be a good girl and remove your clothes, Daddy needs to discipline you for you've been a bad girl." She kicks his crotch and runs up into our bedroom and locks the door. Jack shouts and cusses her.

"You fucking bitch, you slut, let me get my hands on you."

I try to sneak past him but he grabs my hand and pushes me

away from the staircase, "where do you think you're going, I'm not done with you."

I face him and throw a straight punch on his face with all my strength and leave him with a bleeding nose. I run up and bang on the door, "Emma open up, I've punched him and he's down." Before she opens the door, I feel my hair being yanked and pulled; I turn and face a naked Jack standing in front of me, "get down and blow me now!"

I cross my arms and refuse to budge infuriating him even more while Emma opens the door and stands beside me.

"Looks like today is my lucky day, we get to do a threesome, me and my two bitches."

I tell him to get out of our way and let us go but he moves forward, grabs Emma and starts hitting her. I run into the room bring a vase and smash it on his head making him bleed immediately. He turns around, filled with rage and shouts "I will kill you, you fucking bitch. I will kill you both!"

He once again grabs Emma by her hair and flings her around as she screams and cries in pain. Seeing him physically abuse the one person I love, fills me with rage I cannot control. I punch him on the back making him fall on the ground. Both Emma and I start kicking him and push him down the stairs with such force that he hits his head against the wall and falls down unconscious. We take advantage of this and quickly collect our backpacks and run down.

"WAIT, there is something we have to do before we leave, go grab the car keys."

I hurriedly tell Emma who immediately springs into action while I take naked pictures of Jack lying unconscious on the steps.

"Wake up you fucking asshole, wake the fuck up."

I squat next to him and slap him hard enough to wake him. Then stand over him and put my foot on his throat making it hard for him to breathe.

"Listen to me fucker and listen carefully because I will say this once. Emma and I are leaving for good."

He looks like he's about to pass out so I kick him really hard in his groin. His eyes open out wide. I once again put my foot on his throat letting him know that I can do whatever I want with him.

"You make it look like we left after we turned 18, how you do it, is your problem. If you don't, trust me, you and Rhonda will see your naked photos all over the media. We'll email your photos to everyone and tell them what you did to the both of us. And yeah, we will press charges against you. We have proof of everything you've done to us. So, you decide what you want and don't you try to look for us, have I made myself clear?"

He meekly nods his head pleading with me to take my foot of his throat and he gasps for air as soon as I do. Emma kicks him making him whine in pain and spits on him before running out as I start his car and we speed away screaming with joy,

"FREEDOM AT LAST! Here's to an independent, carefree and abuse-free life."

"This is so beautiful - the sunset, the cool breeze and the smell of the sea. Guess this is what freedom looks and smells like."

Emma wraps her arms around her knees as she and I sit on the bonnet of the car overlooking the Pacific Ocean. We've parked the car on the Third Beach in downtown Vancouver before we head to a small motel that we've booked for ourselves till we finalise a rental accommodation.

"I want the time to stop forever as I don't want this dream to end." I sigh and lie down on the hood of the car and look up at the clear sky and the geese flying in a perfect arc.

"I still can't believe we're finally out of that hell hole and free for life."

Emma smiles as she looks at me but in an instant the smile is replaced by a worried look.

"We have taken this step, but how will we live, how will survive – we're not educated enough, who will give us a job."

I sit up face her and look her in the eye.

"What makes you think we won't be able to survive?"

She faces me with tears in her eyes; I smile, wipe her tears and take her hands in mine. "We have an advantage – we are women; we are strong, not only physically but mentally and emotionally. There is nothing in this world that we cannot do if we put our mind to it."

Emma looks confused and uncertain, "after what we've done, who in their right minds will give us a job? What will we do after all the money is over?"

I smile with confidence and pat her cheek.

"The world, my love, is full of weak men who'll do anything to see their stupid fantasies come true and we'll make money off them. We'll do whatever we have to do. We'll do to them what they do to us... We'll use them and then dump them like soiled toilet paper. As long as we are together, no one can do anything to us, we just have to stay together - we'll live good lives I promise you"

Emma finally smiles and says, "Once I finish my education, I'll get into IT... I'm good with programming and I promise you I'll be the best tech person you know."

"I'll need all the tech help I can get and I know I can always count on you. I will destroy Shiv Patel. He messed up my life. He put me in the condition I am – an abused homeless orphan."

"WE NEED to decide what we're going to become. We can't continue with our names and identities. We need a clean break from the past!"

"Nisha is dead. I'm going to change my name to Nalini Shah. I'll get into architecture and interior design. Not because I care about it... but because that fucking asshole Shiv Patel is a real estate magnate who will need a good interior designer. And I'm going to design his interiors to death."

"Well in that case, I'm going to become Carol Smith – the freelance tech girl by day and hacker-for-hire by night!"

I burst out laughing at seeing Emma proclaiming out loudly with great confidence.

"Emma! Speak softly, someone might hear us!"

Emma continues as if she's a queen proclaiming her wishes to her subjects...

"Miss Nalini Shah, who's Emma? I'm Carol Smith! And yeah, I've already checked, there's no one around so no one's going to hear our majestic proclamations!"

We high five each other. I suddenly remember my next task and take out my mobile and get cracking as Carol enjoys the view. Within a few minutes I'm done and smile to myself. I look at Carol who staring at me wondering what I'm up to.

"Now let's make a detailed road map of the next ten years. All the things we need to do."

"Yes, Miss Carol Smith. I agree with you. First, we need to create new identities for ourselves. We need to be officially dead if we really are to start all over again. That will take up thousands of dollars and destroy this car. But because we have taken all of Jack's money and his car along with Rhonda's jewellery, we'll manage."

Carol is curious. "What do you mean all his money? I thought we only took the cash that was lying in their room."

I wink at her. "I found his banking app password and created dozens of cryptocurrency accounts for him and Rhonda and transferred all his money into them. Once we get our new identities, I'll pay someone to convert the money into cash. Then we'll start our own bank accounts and start trading with our own names. Jack won't know what hit him."

Carol laughs. "You're crazy!"

I continue without any hesitation, "Then we'll need to get the fuck out of here. We leave Canada for a few years. Finish our education in the U.S. with our new identities."

Carol is curious, "Then why do we need to come back here? We could simply stay on in the US for the rest of our lives?!"

I look at Carol determined, "No way. We come back here with a plan to finish off Shiv Patel. I'll lay all the groundwork we need to do before we come back here. I don't care what I have to do, but he will pay for what he did."

Carol nods. "By which time we should be millionaires given the way cryptos have been moving up."

I laugh. "Two 17-year-old girls with no formal school education will be millionaires soon! Who would've thought?"

Both Carol and I laugh at how we've been able to manage holding on to our dream. We slide down the hood, get into the car and drive towards what we were determined to turn into a bright, happy future.

I OPEN MY EYES SLOWLY. Still fearful of the horrors that Carol and I have been through. I look around disoriented only to find Carol break open the lock and rush into my room. I'm startled and look at Carol as if wondering why she had to enter like that.

Carol looks at me worried to death.

"What?! I was working on my project when I heard you screaming again in your sleep. I got worried and had to break open the lock. In my panic, I couldn't find my damn key."

I hug Carol and burst into tears. Carol wipes off my tears and finally asks me.

"So what happened in the interview?!"

"I lost big time. Shiv Patel turned out to be far more cunning that I'd ever imagined. It's almost as if he could sense that I was hiding something from him."

"Hold on a minute. Start from the beginning. You walked into the office and then what..."

I look at her trying to remember. She offers me a glass of water and helps me sit up. I look back at her disoriented. "I can't remember!"

Carol looks at me puzzled.

SHIV PATEL WALKS into his den and closes the door. He pours himself a large whiskey and sits down on his favourite couch and lets out a big sigh. He can finally relax for this is the one place where no one can bother him.

The den was a dark room for all purposes and seasons. It had no TV, no internet, no mobile network, no phones, nothing to connect it to the outside world. It was Shiv Patel's man cave and the only place where he could truly be himself.

The Den was out of bounds for everyone, including his own son. No one except an old cleaner was allowed in, and that too because she couldn't hear or speak much. Located in a secret basement in his palatial house, Shiv never allowed anyone else to enter the Den. During his youth, when he had just built his house, he used to call his then girlfriend there for a night of pleasure.

Unfortunately, "the mistress" decided to ask Shiv to double her payment for keeping her mouth shut. Shiv obliged and doubled her pay. And then a month later the mistress – a young twenty-two-year-old was found dead in her bathtub.

Police reports claimed that she had died in an accident when her electric hair dryer had accidentally fallen into the bathtub with her in it. Shiv had to pay his way to get rid of the investigator's suspicions of foul play and since then he didn't allow anyone to enter the room.

There was a small hitch though, the insurance company executive was one nosey persistent woman who decided to tell his wife Alpa Patel about her suspicions regarding the death.

His wife Alpa – an innocent young girl he had married and brought to Canada from his village in western India didn't find his behaviour acceptable. She was appalled to know that there was a record of Shiv having known a man called Adrian Ray who was seen leaving the mistress's building around the same time as her death. Since Adrian Ray was impossible to find and there was no further evidence, they could not press charges against either of them. The young woman's family received the insurance payout as promised by Shiv and kept their mouths shut.

ALPA DECIDED to move out of the house and go back to live with her relatives in India. She had had enough of the lies and his endless affairs. She spoke to Shiv's relatives in Canada and confided the truth to them. While no one had the courage to talk directly to Shiv, rumours had started about his fall from grace.

Shiv decided to put an end to this series of events. He was a highly respected businessman not just in Canada but also in India and couldn't afford any dent in his reputation and popularity. So, Shiv did what he thought he absolutely had to do. He ended the problem.

ALPA'S DEATH had a huge impact on Shiv and he decided to mend his ways. Shiv couldn't let his only son, Neil, suspect any wrong doing on his part and so he consulted the best lawyer that money could buy. His lawyer gave him the best advice he could find – being discreet.

Shiv should discreetly own apartments where he allowed his girlfriends to live rent free and then collect proof of every payment made to them for their services. If any of his numerous girlfriends ever decided to speak out against him, Shiv could easily be defended as a widower who had hired the services of a high-end prostitute. Nothing more than that. This suited Shiv and eased his concerns about protecting his reputation. This also protected his son from finding out what was going on.

Shiv loved Neil and wanted him to have the best of everything. Unfortunately for him, Neil was more like Alpa than him. Always decent, polite and considerate of others.

Shiv had tried to spark the animal instincts in Neil but had failed repeatedly. Neil was a pacifist like his mother and not a ruthless empire builder like Shiv. He felt regret at having had only one child but he tried his best to train Neil to fill the chair he would eventually leave behind.

SHIV IS SUDDENLY JOLTED out of his reverie when his whiskey glass slips out of his hand. He remembers what he had come there for. He quickly opens his secret safe stored under the bed and takes out a folder marked Nisha Shah.

He opens the folder and looks at the photographs inside. Various photos of the young Nisha are kept carefully with dates. He keeps staring at the photos for what seems like eternity. Then Shiv takes out two photos from his coat - one is a photo of the intruder who had entered his office and the other is of Nalini Shah.

He compares all three photos and slams his fist on the glass table shattering it.

Chapter Five

"You haven't lost, you've won! Please don't feel so defeated. I hate seeing you like this!"

Carol tries hard to get me to see the bright side of what in my opinion was a complete disaster.

"I lost my first encounter with my biggest enemy. I prepared myself to face all kinds of adverse circumstances for the last decade. I've repeatedly plunged into troublesome situations, just to teach myself how to gain control of any given situation. And yet, on the first meeting with the Monster, I was reduced to a bumbling blundering incoherent idiot who broke down in front of him."

"You are going to make mistakes Nal. It's inevitable. Just learn to look at the bright side. You don't need this job for the money, you need it only to get inside Shiv's office and become a trusted employee. Also, you may not have got the job, but you still have a good chance. You've got the Monster's son confessing his love to you! What more could you have asked for?"

"He's just a rich playboy wanting to get into bed with me. Let's not kid ourselves. Every woman who has ever dated a rich man has the same story to tell. It begins with the flowers and the gifts and promises of undying love. And soon within six months to a year the rich guy gets bored of the woman and gently eases her out of his life. We've seen this happen so many times."

"What if it isn't? What if this time it is different? Why would a rich playboy publicly confess his feelings for you? If he just wanted you in bed, he could have found a way to meet you privately and seduced you. Why confess his feelings openly and make himself available to public scrutiny?"

CAROL ALWAYS HAS a way to look at the positive in any situation. And yet I know for a fact that she worries about things much more than I do. I'm a skydiver, so I take risks and plunge into the unknown without thinking too much. Carol is a worrier and so she plans for everything in minute detail. The two of us together have overcome the most difficult of situations but this stalemate with Shiv Patel seems different.

"Shiv knows something. He has a way of getting under my skin, he suspects that I'm the intruder. And the way he caught on to my being uncomfortable about a background check tells me that he probably suspects I'm not Nalini but Nisha – the young kid whose parents he killed."

"Okay. Let us for a moment assume that you're right. Okay? Now what is he going to do? A background-check? Let him do it. Once he's done with the background check, his suspicions will die out. Point is, by then if you don't play your cards well, you'll be out of the game!"

"So, what do you think I should do?"

Carol picks up a profile of Neil Patel that she's created by accessing all the social media accounts and all the information we had on him and waves it at me.

"This guy. He's your door into the company. Once you're in, everything will start working according to plan again. That's all you need. All you have to do is seduce one guy, without letting him know that you're the one leading him on. Come on! You've fooled so many men into believing that you're in love with them, this guy isn't so different, is he?"

I look at Carol and nod. I understand the soundness of her logic. She's usually right about most things.

Carol continues making her point and says "Women who have aspired for power and influence have used everything and everyone available to them, to get what they want. So, get on with it, because you're smarter than most of them."

I smile at Carol. Being a high IQ, anti-social, analytical, loner may have some limitations, but if she's by your side, you can wage war with the devil. She looks at me relaxing and exhales loudly. Then goes to the kitchen and gets me a coffee and some muffins. As both of us stare out of the window at the nothing in particular lost in our own thoughts, Carol notices someone on the road.

"There! There he is!"

I rush to look at the road down below and see Neil arriving in his playboy sports-car and parking it outside my building. Carol pushes me back into the room and points to the phone. Just then the phone rings. It's Neil calling me at 8 am.

"Now do you believe me?!" asks Carol.

I'm about to take the call when Carol screams...

"Let it ring out! Don't take the call."

"What if he comes up?"

"He won't. He's in love with you. He won't do anything to make you uncomfortable."

Carol seems to have got it right. Neil keeps calling but doesn't get out of his car.

The phone keeps ringing persistently like a stubborn child, bent upon fulfilling their wish and I like a seasoned parent ignore it successfully.

Ultimately in this tug of war, the phone gives up and all that is left are five missed calls.

Two hours later, at 10 am I call back Mr. Playboy-with-kind-eyes-and-a-dreamy-voice Neil Patel. I put the phone on speaker so that Carol can also listen.

Neil begs me to meet him for a coffee.

"Go for coffee! Go go go.... Do not let go of this opportunity" Carol whispers super excited and almost says it out loud!

I say yes to Neil and promise to meet him at the local Tim Horton's for coffee in 10 minutes.

As soon as I cut the call, Carol holds me by my shoulders and shakes me as she screams in excitement. She pushes me towards the window and both of us look at Neil getting out of the car looking all happy and cheerful. The moment he looks in our direction, we duck and hide behind our plants, with Carol almost falling on top of me.

I see Neil standing wearing a crisp white semi-formal shirt with blue semi-formal trousers, smiling at no one in particular.

Carol gives out an "Awwww..." without even being aware of it.

To be honest, I'm actually quite turned on at the moment. Just thinking of the connection Neil and I had shared in the few moments we spent together makes me want to be with him. Carol puts her arms around me waking me up from my daydreams and bringing me back to reality.

"I know you have a thing for him and that you are falling for him, but my love, do not let your emotions control you. Right now, you need to go for coffee with him, woo him on to your side and get the damn job!"

I realise that this would mean cheating on Neil's seemingly innocent feelings for me, but I don't care. Carol is right. I need to get things lined up so that when the time comes, I can turn the situation in any direction I want. We give a high five to each other as I mumble to myself, "Let the games begin – Shiv Patel start counting your days."

Carol rushes back and starts working on her laptop while I walk out of our apartment.

Neil is sitting on the patio of the Tim Hortons cafe soaking in the sun, looking like a model, fresh out of a Vogue magazine cover.

"Beautiful day, eh." I say out aloud as I walk up to him smiling ear to ear as if someone's stuffed a hanger in my mouth. He stands up and all I can think of is to wrap my arms and legs around him as he lifts me up and then kiss him for eternity.

Instead I shake his hand and sit on the chair across from him. It's hard for me to take my eyes off him.

"What would you like to have – an ice cap, frosty, ice frappe or just regular coffee?"

"Regular coffee with something to munch on please."

He smiles and rubs his palm on my shoulder as walks into the café to place the order.

'The Date' as I would like to call it goes well with us casually flirting with each other. Neil tries begging and pleading with me to accept the idea of working in Variety, despite his Dad's misbehaviour.

"I am very sorry for what happened and trust me, you'll really enjoy working with me."

"Are we here to talk about the job or..."

Neil is taken aback by my directness.

"To me the job is just the beginning Nalini. I want you with me at all times. I want to spend every waking hour with you."

"Oh, so you don't want me with you when you're asleep?!"

Both of us burst into laughter. I smile as I see the sincerity in his eyes. He isn't lying. He genuinely feels what he's saying.

"Will you please say yes and accept the job if I get you a formal written offer?"

I take my time as I don't want to appear too eager.

"Please say yes Nalini. Just this once, agree to what I'm saying and if things don't work out, you can always quit after the six-month-probation is over. Please?!"

I finally smile and nod in agreement.

"Okay. I'll accept the idea of a six-month-probation and if I don't enjoy it, I will quit!"

Neil doesn't seem to be able to contain his joy. He puts his

WHAT COMES FROM WITHIN

hand on mine, looks into my eyes as he comes close and kisses me on my lips. Just like that!

We get involved with each other.

No grand merry go round, no fussing, no flowers, nothing. Just instant attraction and unimaginable chemistry.

I don't know what overcomes me when I'm with him. So, I too give in to the vibe of the moment. I don't resist his kiss and reciprocate by giving him a long lingering kiss. It's like we're both locked in an eternal dance of love between two soulmates.

There is something magical about the first kiss, the first touch, the first everything. Neil is like a kid wanting more but I move away from him. He smiles at me.

"That was the best kiss I've ever had."

He keeps looking into my eyes and I too look back. Both of us are locked in a gaze as if just that much is enough to know each other and commit our lives to each other.

Neil wants to say something and so do I but it seems as if we'll destroy the moment we're having together so neither of us say anything.

Finally, after what feels like hours of looking into each other's eyes, Neil can't contain his joy...

"Do you want to go to my apartment and chill for some time? It will give us some time together and..."

I know where this is going and regain my composure very quickly. I desperately want to be in his arms and kiss him again but I cannot. This is too important.

"Let's take things slowly lover boy! I'll be waiting to receive the formal job offer from you."

I get up to leave because I know that if I stay there for longer, I will end up in his bedroom in no time. Neil looks disappointed.

As I'm walking away I turn and look back. He's still staring at me with lovelorn eyes.

"I've applied to other firms as well and I've decided to take the first good offer I get so I do hope that your formal job offer comes soon."

Neil face turns from a kid who loves his candy and wants to eat more – to the kid who might lose out on all the candy in the world for all times to come.

I let out a gentle laugh as a I walk away from him.

It is 1 in the afternoon and both Carol and I have been sitting inside our car, parked outside Stephanie Milton's apartment building for the last half hour.

There is a nip in the air and sky is overcast, "I smell rain." Carol looks towards the skies and crinkles her nose as I zoom in with my phone camera.

"Oh look, there is Shiv's car going into the parking lot." Carol screams and I put a hand on her mouth to shut her up, "we are in hiding, stop yelling and getting attention."

I start recording the video of Shiv walk into Stephanie's apartment on my phone.

We turn on the listening device we've planted inside Stephanie's house to hear their conversation. Carol is on the phone with Stephanie who has a modified Bluetooth device stuck inside her left ear that she's covered with her perfect hair.

Carol whispers into the phone... "Stay calm Stephanie! You're a winner. You can do this!"

Stephanie looks scared as she sees Shiv look around suspiciously. Stephanie tries to put up a fake smile for Shiv. Shiv notices this.

"How have you been? Sorry I couldn't come last weekend, was stuck up at work. Did you get the money?" Shiv takes off his coat and kisses Stephanie who looks very uncomfortable. Shiv looks at her suspiciously.

"Stephanie, everything alright?!"

"Steph, act normal!" I say to her and instantly her expressions change and she's at ease.

"Yes. Everything's okay. What would you like to have?"

Stephanie says to Shiv who settles comfortably on the couch and turns on the television.

"I'll have a nice hot coffee and a sandwich."

As soon as Stephanie goes into the kitchen, Shiv immediately gets up and comes to the window. He looks around curiously and both of us are forced to duck and hide inside the car to avoid being seen by him.

It's uncanny how Shiv has a sixth sense about everything that could be disadvantageous to him. After looking around and being satisfied that no one is looking into the apartment, Shiv hears Stephanie walking back towards him and he immediately goes back to the couch and pretends to watch TV. Stephanie brings him his coffee and a sandwich.

Carol tells Stephanie to start with making casual conversation about him and Neil.

Stephanie asks Shiv about how Neil has been doing. Shiv relaxes on seeing Stephanie being herself with him. As he sips his coffee, he starts getting into the flow of the conversation with Stephanie.

Stephanie, I must say, is an excellent actor when directed properly. He continues to watch TV as he sips on his coffee. Stephanie goes and sits next to him. She looks at him lovingly as Shiv takes her hand and puts it on his chest.

"Stephanie, go for it!" Carol directs her softly but firmly and instantly we hear Stephanie's voice booming.

"Shiv, I need to talk to you and I cannot do it with the TV blaring, so I will turn it off and I need your undivided attention." With that she promptly shuts off the TV and leans forward. She puts her face on Shiv's chest and gently moves her fingers across his body. Shiv doesn't understand where this is going but Stephanie is determined to take things forward just as we had planned.

Stephanie sighs loudly, takes the cup from his hand and places it away from him.

"I have something to tell you and I want you to be compassionate and understanding of me. Please don't get angry at me."

Shiv looks at her curiously, waiting for her to speak up. Another deep breadth and she lets loose.

"Shiv, I'm pregnant with your child and I cannot raise it on my own, so we have to get married."

Shiv looks like he's seen a ghost, "You what?!" He shouts and springs up from the couch and stands in front of Stephanie, towering over her and glaring as if he would kill her in an instant.

"Don't get scared, Steph. Remember we are here, we're recording everything so if anything goes wrong, there will be a cop in no time."

These words seem to have a magical effect on her. We are surprised to see her stand tall in front of him and say out aloud, "I'm pregnant and the sooner you accept it, the better it will be for us." She looks disgusted with his reaction and pushes him aside almost making him trip and walks towards a small corner table. "I knew this is how you would react so I got you proof. This is the sonogram image of our baby."

Shiv looks like he's been punched in the gut. He looks at the sonogram and slumps on the couch. Carol and I smile, "Well done."

Shiv sits in silence staring at the image; Stephanie goes and sits next to him, places her hand on his leg and points at the image, "this is our baby."

Shiv continues to stare and then says, "Get it aborted, we don't need that thing and the sooner you get it done, the better it is. Am I clear?" Stephanie looks appalled,

"Why would you say something like that? This is our child, we created it and no way am I aborting it – now am I clear?"

Shiv sighs and tries to put his arm around but Stephanie brushes it away glaring back at him, "all this time all you've done is use me for sex and now because I am carrying your child you have the nerve to ask me to abort it. I am keeping this baby, whether you like it or not."

Shiv stands up and starts pacing. Carol and I are enjoying ourselves thoroughly.

Our trainee has outdone herself. "I'm pretty sure, he's sweating." I try to zoom in to his face on my phone camera. Carol shushes me, "Shush, he's saying something and I can't hear clearly."

She cranks up the volume on the listening device and Shiv's booming voice comes on and I see him sit in front of her, take her hands in his, as he says, "Listen, I know you're overwhelmed and most of it is because of the hormones, but I've always loved you, trust me. This is the best relationship I've had, even better than my marriage and no, I'm not with you for sex – I can get that anytime I want. So please, don't ruin this beautiful relationship we have by filling it with diapers, feeding bottles and baby clothes. Let's get rid of this thing and start all over again."

He leans forward to kiss her, but she pushes him away. We watch in amazement as Stephanie takes her cue to try and make a deal with him.

"Mr. Patel, get this straight. I am not aborting this baby and now, I want the biggest solitaire you can get me, a huge engagement party where the who's who of Vancouver invited as guests and 50% partnership in Variety."

She pokes her index finger in his chest before walking away from him and says, "Now, put that coffee cup of yours in the dishwasher and you can show yourself out."

Carol and I gasp as we did not expect this from her, "She's brilliant! I never thought she would say all that and so strongly." Carol says in amazement as I continue to watch with my mouth open. "Oh, hey looks like he's begging her."

We watch as Stephanie looks disgusted and angry with Shiv and walks off into her bedroom. Shiv can't believe this is happening. His carefully crafted public image, his reputation as a respectable industry leader, the endless questions from the media and international tabloids, everything in his life would fall apart if he didn't control this situation. He instinctively follows her into the bedroom. I quickly adjust my phone camera and point it towards the bedroom whose windows have been kept wide open for our benefit.

Shiv continues trying to convince her to abort the baby, "hey honey listen, I'll give you anything you want but only if you abort it. See we both love each other and why ruin what we have – trust me it's not worth it, I've gone through it and I am saying this from experience."

Stephanie breaks down and says, "you already have a child but I want one and no, I am not aborting. Why don't you understand?"

He puts his hands on her arms and turns her towards him, "What do you want, tell me. I'll do everything I can to convince you." He says softly as she turns her face away not wanting to look him in the eye – that would give her game away. She closes her eyes tightly, sighs, breaks free from his hold and crosses her arms around her chest.

"I want to marry you – I deserve to be called your wife. A proper millionaire's wife. Is that asking for a lot?" She takes out a picture of them together in the bed, naked and smooching, "This is what I want for life – I want to be Mrs. Stephanie Patel; there I said it."

Shiv clenches his teeth, runs his hands through his hair and walks out of the room.

"You're doing good – just keep at it." Carol encourages Stephanie and I grab the head set from her, "Listen Stephanie, if he tries to negotiate just stick to your demand for a marriage!"

I hear Shiv coming back and hand the headset to Carol while I focus on getting everything recorded on the phone camera.

"Let's make a deal – I get you an Ocean and Mountain View villa in either North Van or West Van, a million dollars in your bank account and we end this relationship, right here, right now. Once this deal is done, you and I have nothing to do with each other, we never knew each other and this child in you is not mine – is that a deal?" Shiv raises his eyebrows as he looks at Stephanie closely monitoring her expressions. "Don't bend down – stick to getting married to him." Carol directs her and I see her walking past him as she says, "All I want is to be married to you; is that asking for too much? And what makes you think that I'm for sale, that you can throw some money at me and buy me off? Why don't you man up and marry me?"

As she storms out of the bedroom, she is followed by an enraged Shiv who grabs her arm, turns her around and puts his hand on her throat in an attempt to strangulate her; Stephanie screams in fear.

"Call the cop now!" I yell to Carol, who whips out her phone and quickly dials a number, "Hey, can you go in? It looks like he's strangling her."

Shiv pins Stephanie against the wall with his hand on her neck, pushing her further down as she kicks her legs and fight to breathe, "you fucking bitch. I have taken a lot of shit from you and Shiv Patel never takes shit from anyone. As far as the law is concerned, you're just a high-end whore who is staying in my property rent-free and getting paid for the services you provide me. That's all! So, you can't blackmail me. Do you understand?!"

She scrambles hard to free herself from his grip but he is strong for his age. She manages to let out another scream.

"A cop is on his way Stephanie, so fight and stay strong."

Just then her doorbell rings. Shiv is immediately alarmed. Shiv loosen his grip on her as he fiercely whispers, "you say a word about us to anyone and I'll make sure you disappear. You understand me?"

Shiv pushes a visibly shaken Stephanie towards the door.

Stephanie opens the door to find her elderly neighbour, Doug inquiring about her wellbeing.

"All well in here, I heard some screaming – you ok, love?"

Stephanie looks nervous but holds her ground and tells Doug that she and her boyfriend are watching a movie, which had a violent scene, and all is well in her apartment. Doug looks at her, then at Shiv.

"I know him from somewhere. He's that real estate million-aire; isn't he?!"

Stephanie nods. Doug looks at Stephanie disappointed, as if he didn't expect her to have an ageing man for a boyfriend then leaves.

She closes the door, turns around to face Shiv with a smirk on her face, "so where were we, Mr. Patel?" She sounds sarcastic and Shiv walks towards her knowing that since the neighbour has seen him in her apartment – she can file charge against him and use the neighbour as a witness.

Shiv immediately changes track; "I'm sorry, I just lost control of my emotions. I'll give you whatever you want – just name it, although I can't marry you, I will ensure that you and your child will have a lavish lifestyle and I will pay for it. I will transfer funds for child support and the child's education."

As we watch them, our cop friend parks his car and rushes into the building.

While Shiv and Stephanie are having their discussion, the doorbell rings again, "God damn it, who is it this time?" Shiv flings opens the door, irritated, only to see a cop, "Sir, we've had a complaint about some violent noises here. Is everything okay?"

Shiv stammers, "All well officer, nothing violent happening here. We were just relaxing."

The cop looks past Shiv and sees Stephanie on the couch crying and says, "mind if I come in and ask a few routine questions?"

Shiv lets him in and stands behind Stephanie as the cop sits across from her and asks her, "Ma'am, is everything ok?" He notices Shiv standing behind Stephanie and asks him to leave the room.

Shiv hesitates but eventually steps out into the patio. The cop asks a few questions to Stephanie who confirms that they were just watching a violent film and the volume was high which could have caused the neighbours to think that something was happening in her apartment. The cop nods and gestures to Shiv to come in. Before leaving the cop says to Shiv, "She has bruise marks on her neck and her wrist. That doesn't happen from watching action movies. I've made a note of that. I'm leaving at the moment but rest assured, I will be watching and monitoring you."

Our cop friend leaves. Shiv stares at her after slamming the front door. He stands tall in front of her; legs apart and hands on the hips. Stephanie sighs, shakes her head.

"I'm so disappointed in you Shiv! I never expected you to hurt me like this!"

Shiv is well past caring for her feelings. He's like a wounded lion who has been cornered. He grabs her wrist and twists it. Then asks her menacingly... "Do we have a deal?! You get a villa in North-Van, a million dollars for aborting the child and ending our relationship. You will never speak about me ever again for the rest of your life. Agreed?!" Stephanie nods even as she winces in pain.

Shiv lets go of her arm. Stephanie runs into the bedroom and slams the door shut.

Shiv heaves, looks tired and defeated as he collects his coat before leaving the apartment. We keep the phone camera pointed at him, capturing the video of Shiv leaving the apartment and then going away in his car. After a few seconds of him leaving, I finally end shooting the video and rush into the apartment to meet Stephanie.

Meanwhile our cop friend comes out and meets Carol only to see that she has tears in her eyes. He is taken aback, "Hey, are you okay?"

Carol tries to regain her composure and nods Yes.

The cop comes forward and holds her hand. "Bad memories?!"

Carol clears her throat and says, "Yes. Both Nal and I have suffered a lot. We just wanted to help this girl. Please make a report about what you saw so that if anything does go wrong, we can use it in the future."

The cop gently rubs her hand with his palm. "Will do! Will you be okay?"

Carol nods and gives him a quick hug. "Thank you, if you hadn't been there for us today, he might have killed her."

The Cop nods, "Sure no problem. It's my job and duty." He hesitates and then asks carol, "Do you want to meet up later for a coffee... "

Carol finally smiles. "Yes, I've been wanting to since I first saw you! Pick me up at 7 this evening. I'll text you the address."

The cop smiles and leaves.

Stephanie looks totally disheveled as she opens the door to her apartment. It's obvious that she didn't expect Shiv to be the complete monster we had warned her about.

Stephanie hugs me as she breaks down and cries. She's got bruise marks on her neck, her shoulder and her wrist. I quickly take photos of everything to keep a record of what had happened.

"Now you finally understand what I was talking about?"

Stephanie nods as she tries to overcome the shock of Shiv's threat to kill her.

"Don't worry. You're almost done. Now I'm sure Shiv will transfer the property and the money to you very quickly. And once that is done, we will help you sell the property, take your money and leave the country for good. Once you're out of Shiv's reach, you can restart your life."

Stephanie says "Thank God. I'll be happy to get rid of this psycho. I deserve better."

I give her a quick hug and leave.

On the way back home, Carol who is driving looks at me with an are-you-okay look.

I finally exhale. "Well that ended well!"

Carol who is much more analytical says "We did it – she out of the picture and cannot do anything to ruin our plan. Time to celebrate. Oh, and I have to prepare for tonight."

Carol and I fist bump each other – we're happy, tired but exhilarated.

Meanwhile, Shiv is driving back home. He regrets assaulting Stephanie. He knows that he's made a mistake and that he has to pay a price for it. He knows that it was a set up but can't figure out how Stephanie did it. If he as much as looks at her and breathes in her direction, she could file assault charges against him and get him arrested. She has two witnesses - a neighbour who's heard screams and seen her with him. And a cop who has noticed the bruise marks.

A simple written complaint from Stephanie could destroy his reputation and he would become a standing joke on national television. Shiv calmly weighs the odds and finally decides to pay up because it's the least risky thing to do. He searches for his phone, and then speed dials a number.

"Edward, I need you to talk to our lawyers and prepare transfer documents for the villa in North Van. I also want you to take out a million dollars in cash and keep it ready. Also get Stephanie to sign that non-disclosure agreement."

Edward says "Okay boss."

Shiv is angry at himself but can't speak about it so he vents it out on Edward.

"Speak up you idiot! I can't hear you. I want this done at the earliest and at top priority, so leave everything and get to it."

I change into my nightwear, garb a bottle of wine with a bag of chips and settle comfortably under the comforter on my couch and put on a web series, when Carol walks into the living room holding two dresses, a blood red and a midnight blue – both deep necked, lacy and a bit transparent, "which one of these says, 'come to mama'?" I raise my eyebrows in amusement and smile.

I lazily point at the midnight blue and tell her to enhance her eyes, "put on subtle makeup and do smoky eyes and oh, less jewellery – remember less is always more."

She disappears into her bedroom to get dressed while I continue with my wine and web series. Almost 45 minutes later

Carol emerges from the bedroom and my jaw drops, "Look at you, you look like a film star. Get ready, Mr. Cop Man for some jail time with the prettiest woman in town." I whistle making her blush, something she doesn't do very often. She walks across the room and I can't take my eyes off her, I wonder how that cop will hold himself; I smile at this thought – it's good to see my best friend happy. She paces back and forth occasionally checking the clock

"It's almost 7, where the hell is he?"

"Relax, he'll come. Sit down and have a glass of wine with me." I slur a bit and she shakes her head and continues walking when her cell phone rings loudly, "Hi Kevin, oh you've reached. Great. I'll just come down." I clear my throat as she ends the call, "Kevin? Nice name. I'm happy for you and I really hope it works out for you." I give her a quick hug and wave goodbye to her knowing she will not be coming back tonight.

SHIV TAKES the local Sky Train dressed in a long, black overcoat and a hat and gets off at the Granville Station from where he walks all the way to East Hastings Street, infamously known as the Druggee Street, as it is home to the homeless addicted to drugs. He walks cautiously looking around him as people fight with each other over drugs and food; it is almost as if he does not want to be here and is feeling out of place.

Shiv dials Adrian's phone but it goes straight to voicemail so he leaves a message.

"Adrian, I'm here. Call me when you get this message."

Within seconds, he gets a location pin on his phone. Shiv follows the directions and goes into a dingy shanty Chinese restaurant where he finds Adrian sitting alone in a darkened corner. There is no one else in the restaurant and Shiv feels uncomfortable with the ambience. He quickly goes over to Adrian's table and sits opposite him.

Adrian doesn't say anything. He just pushes a file in front of

Shiv. Shiv opens the file and looks inside. He looks perplexed. "How is this possible?" he mumbles.

"Are you absolutely sure that Nalini and Nisha are not the same person?" asks Shiv.

Adrian nods. "Nisha Shah and her friend Emma – two 17-year-olds died in a car accident eight years ago. You can see the photos of the charred bodies there."

Adrian points to the photos of two burnt corpses.

Shiv looks at them as if trying to decipher what might have happened.

Adrian continues "Nalini Shah finished her education in the US. She just moved to Canada some four years ago. I've double checked all the degrees. They're authentic. Nalini Shah is not Nisha Shah. That much is clear."

Shiv looks baffled and shakes his head in denial. "How is it even possible?"

He takes out the photos of Nisha, Nalini and the intruder and shows them to Adrian. Says "Just look at these. Don't all three of these appear to be the same person?"

Adrian looks at the photos and nods. "They do. But everything in Nalini Shah's resume checks out."

Shiv whispers, head bent and in denial. He rubs his eyes; he is tired and sighs loudly, "Dig deeper, Adrian, I still have a very strong feeling that she is the same girl."

Adrian nods, "I thought about all the possible angles. How could a 17-year-old orphan girl with no family, no support, no job or income have escaped her foster parents and faked her death in Vancouver. Then created a fake Canadian identity, then gone to the U.S., completed her Graduate degree there, then come back here and finished her Master's degree? It's not possible!"

Shiv shakes his head in disgust. It's almost as if he's losing the battle to a helpless orphan girl. He just can't believe that it's not the same girl. He looks at Adrian determined to prove that his hunch is right.

"But what if this girl did fake her death? What if this girl did manage to create a fake identity? If there is no wrong doing on her part, then why was she so wary of taking about her background and her parents? Why did she break down during her interview?!"

"She was abandoned by her illegal immigrant Indian parents in the U.S. She's lived and done temp jobs her whole life. She has worked her way up. She did get a full scholarship for her Master's degree. It's all true."

"Then what is she doing here in Vancouver? Why did she shift base to Canada? Why apply for a job in Variety? Why not stay back in the U.S. and work there? It doesn't make sense.

"It could be because she's had a bad relationship. A breakup. People leave their home country for a variety of reasons. There's nothing suspicious in that."

"Dammit!" Shiv looks frustrated.

Adrian wonders why Shiv is so obsessed with the girl, Nisha. It's almost as if she's an adversary he is scared of! Shiv finally looks at Adrian determined to get to the bottom of the story. "Get me irrefutable proof that this identity – this Nalini Shah identity is solid. Check in every nook and corner of this identity. Find out where she lived, who she lived with, who she hung out with, find out everything! I want a complete timeline of Nalini Shah's life. I want to know everything about her. I want to be absolutely certain!"

Adrian decides to offer his boss the most expensive of services. "If you're so apprehensive and worried, why not just take her out? She could die the same way your mistress died."

Shiv shakes his head. "No. There is something fishy going on here. This girl Nalini Shah is well connected. I gave you her resume, she's done pro-bono work for the government and its agencies – both in Canada and the U.S. She knows people and is possibly in touch with them. Her resume is her way of informing me that I can't touch her without drawing attention to myself. I can't take the risk of being investigated again right now. If she is Nisha Shah, then she's played her cards really well. Doing all the things she's done takes a lot of time and planning. So, until I

know everything, I won't take any decision on what to do with
her. Get me all the proof I need."

Shiv gets up and leaves. Adrian picks up the photos of Nisha
Shah and Nalini Shah and compares the two. Maybe Shiv is right.
They certainly look like the same person.

It is 10:30 pm and Shiv Patel is back in his office. He stands
alone looking at the Vancouver skyline, hands in his pockets, legs
wide apart and a grim look on his face. The entire city is lit up and
glistening like small zircons on a large black canvas. He remembers
the way Adrian was surprised at his apprehensions about Nalini
Shah. Adrian had never seen him being so worried about any one
person the way he was worried about this one girl.

Shiv chides himself for showing his vulnerability to Adrian.
He knew that sooner rather than later, Adrian would up his price
for doing all the dirty work. Shiv regrets displaying his weakness
to Adrian. Then wonders why he was reacting this way. Were the
demons of his past finally catching up with him?

He had killed four people by now, besides his own wife and
mistress. All that work was done by Adrian. But he had never
been worried about any of them the way he worried about this
Nalini or Nisha, whoever she was. This girl seemed to be different.
There was something about her – a single mindedness that
reminded him of how he used to be himself when he was younger.

Shiv takes a deep breath as he decides that he's not going to be
impulsive. That he's going to play his cards really well. Just as he
calms himself down, Neil walks into his office. "Dad, where were
you all day?"

Neil looks worried and places his hand on Shiv's shoulder,
"what's up pop? Share with me, what is bothering you. Come on,
let me fix you a drink and let's chat."

He pats Shiv's back in a friendly way before moving to the
small mini bar by the couch and pours an expensive scotch in two

crystal glasses and hands one to Shiv who sits heavily on the couch. "This is the first time since your mother passed away that I've felt so alone and vulnerable; didn't realise how much I miss her – she was my best friend, I could share anything with her at any time."

He slowly sips his scotch and smacks his lips enjoying it. Neil looks concerned – he did not realise how fast his father had aged; Shiv does look tired and defeated.

They sit and talk for an hour like old friends, having scotch and catching up on old times when Shiv finally says, "guess we should be heading out son, it's getting late and I'm not getting any younger; I need my full eight-hour sleep." He places his glass on the side table, gets up, puts on his coat and gets ready to leave.

Neil walks up to him, helps him with his coat, "Dad, I need to talk to you; just give me a few minutes please." Shiv turns and faces him, "If you are here to advocate about that girl Nalini Shah; I've made up my mind and don't want to hear another word."

He picks up his bag and makes his way towards the door when Neil comes in front of him and blocks him; pleading with him to listen, "I know you have your reasons but please listen to what I have to say before you make a final decision."

Shiv looks at him angrily. Neil holds him by his shoulder and manoeuvres him back to the couch, "it won't be long, for once please listen to reason. I don't want you to take any decision in haste." Shiv shrugs his hand away and shouts, "What do you think I am Neil? What makes you think that I don't have the ability to make good decisions?"

Shiv leans forward and pokes Neil in the chest with his index finger, "Don't teach me how to run my firm and don't forget, I am the CEO and your father. My decision stands as is and nothing will make me change it." He tries to walk away but Neil holds his hand and gives him a desperate look, "Dad please, just listen to me for once." Shiv sighs in surrender and slumps on the couch, "go on and make it fast." Neil pulls a chair and sits across from him, "Dad, I understand you have your apprehensions but at least give her a chance; Her personal life has nothing to do with her work and I feel we were being too harsh on her at the interview. For my sake just give her a chance and if she does not perform, I'll be the first person to kick her out of this office."

Shiv looks straight at him without blinking and then leans back on the couch as Neil continues, "Let's make a deal dad, let's not give her a permanent position instead let's bring her on-board on a six-month probation and watch how she does and if she does not perform or anything else, we can fire her without cause."

Shiv's initial reluctance gives way to a more thoughtful stance. He understands the advantage of keeping Nalini Shah under his watchful eye. This way she will be accessible to him at all times. He would be able to monitor what she is up to while Adrian gathers more information about her. She won't have the time to create any more fake documents or defend herself. He wonders why he didn't think of this earlier.

Shiv pretends to give in to Neil's thinking and nods in agreement, "Fine, you've presented your case well. Tell her to come onboard on probation starting Monday, now can I go home and rest for the night?" Shiv heaves as he gets up from the couch. Neil hugs him tightly, "thank you thank you thank you – I promise, you will not regret it."

Shiv smiles as he says, "I'm going to load her with a whole lot of work. Let's see how good she is."

Neil says "Done! Give her all the work you want done. I'll personally supervise her and make sure that she does everything you want."

Shiv walks out of the office with a grin on his face. He finally feels that he's one move ahead of her.

I'M ABOUT to head to bed when my phone starts ringing relentlessly, "Hi Neil, what a surprise, what made you call at this hour?" I try to sound surprised although I've figured out the reason for the call. He tells me that I've been hired and I would need to come down to the office to sign the employment agreement soon. I smile to myself as I hear these words come out of my mouth, "I can't wait to start; I'll be there on Monday. Have a good night, see you soon."

I am about to hang up when Neil says, "Hey, when can we meet? I'm dying to meet you!"

I quiet down for a moment before responding, "Take it easy playboy. Let me get started with work and get into the rhythm of things at Variety. Over time we'll get to know each other and figure out if we're compatible or not."

I hear him chuckle on the other end; wish him goodnight with a promise to meet him in the office on Monday and cut the call. I'm too drunk to figure out what's happening with me. Part of me just wants to use Neil to achieve my goals but there's another part of me that knows that the connection with him is real.

I know that I'm conflicted and don't know why. Things were absolutely clear to me when I started this mission. And now that I'm finally making some progress, I'm beginning to hesitate. Things weren't supposed to happen this way. I wasn't planning on falling in love and yet this is where I am. I don't know which way things are headed with Neil. I hope I don't let my feelings for Neil destroy what I've put in place over the last 15 years. I sigh as I put my head on the pillow and shut my eyes.

Some days it's just best to sleep it off. Tomorrow is another day!

There is a nip in the air but I still curl up on the oval patio swing watching the sunrise, throwing a golden glow on the windows of the nearby high rises. I woke up early today because I wanted to spend some time alone before the Big Day.

It's a beautiful day with clear blue skies, crisp breeze and an out of the world sunrise but nothing is helping my mood; I am very emotional today, "It's my first day at work. How I wish, you were here. If only, I could do something to bring you both back. I so want to hug you and never let you go.... Please come back, Mum, Dad..."

I say a silent prayer and pull the warm comforter closer watching the city come to life with cars lining up on the roads, people thronging cafes to get their first cup of coffee before starting their day and train stations packed with unwilling workers forced to go to work.

I take in a deep breath as if soaking in the sun along with its raw energy and vitality. I will need all the strength I can get. I know why Shiv Patel has agreed to hire me. It's like they say, keep your friends close and your enemies closer.

Carol walks in just in time and keeps her promise of dropping me to my office on my first day at work at Variety. We grab coffee from a Tim Hortons drive through and Carol zips through the Monday traffic on the roads and reach Variety in the nick of time. I wave her goodbye and take a deep breath as I look at the building and everything its owner represents - an unquenchable thirst for power, tremendous wealth, a huge network of influential friends, total disregard for the law and a complete lack of basic human decency. The fact that I've survived Shiv's numerous attempts to break me and destroy my spirit is in itself a miracle. And I won't let that miracle go waste. Someday I will own this building and change everything it stands for.

But first I have to destroy the Monster who own it – Shiv Patel!

Chapter Six

The place is thronging with people clad in business suits, holding laptop bags and talking endlessly on their phones. It's like a sea of black overcoats in a narrow corridor with elevators on either side waiting impatiently to get into one and start yet another day – another week.

I scramble into an elevator and get off on the 23rd floor of the Variety Real Estate office. I take a selfie against Variety's board making a 'V' with my fingers before entering the office and send it to Carol who responds with a thumbs-up emoji and a "Stick to the Plan" message.

"Hi, I've been hired as an intern."

The same brunette in her business casual pencil skirt rules the reception area and gestures to me to wait as she answers the phone.

I walk towards the slanting windows and take in the breath-taking view of the majestic Northern mountains.

"Nalini Shah" the brunette stands behind me and gestures to me to follow her as she shows me my work desk. "So, this is going to be your work station. You will shortly be taken in for training, if you want coffee there is a café at the end of the room and if you need anything, you know where to find me. I'm Sarah, by the way." She smiles and walks back to the reception as I start settling into my new space, which is a small cubicle connected with other desks, just like the ones in a contact centre. I have a small tote under my hydraulic standing desk in which I put my hand bag along with a small recorder.

Before I can get a sense of the office space, the phone on my desk rings. I pick it up half expecting it to be Neil, but it isn't. It's Shiv Patel calling me to his cabin urgently. I keep all my stuff aside and rush into his cabin.

As I enter his cabin, I try and focus my mind to take in the entire space of the office. Although I've been there before, I will need to know everything about the office so that I can get in and get out quickly. I look around memorising everything I can see and creating a visual map in my head.

There is probably a safe or a document locker hidden behind the painting that is just slightly tilted. I look around while Shiv is busy barking orders into his phone. His office feels a bit heated so there is probably some central air conditioning vent somewhere although it doesn't seem to be visible right now. There are some books on the shelf behind him. They haven't changed position since the first time I sneaked into this office. So, they're probably just for show. I don't think he's the kind that takes time out to read books.

There is something eerily wrong about the office although I can't quite figure it out. Shiv finishes his phone call and looks at me. I keep standing because he hasn't asked me to sit. We look at each other for a long moment. It's as if Shiv is assessing the best way to handle me while I'm figuring out the best way to outwit him. It's a game of cat and mouse.

The interview was his day. Getting Stephanie to screw him over was my day.

Although he doesn't know all this yet, but I'm sure some day he will. He's too smart and clever to stay in the dark for long. Now that I'm one of his employees, I suppose today is his turn to play the game.

Shiv finally clears his throat and says in his deep booming voice, "I hope you know that you aren't here for your good looks."

I stand straight in front of him letting him know that I'm up for a fight if he wants one. I reply back curtly, "Yes. I'm aware that this is an office and I'm here to work. So, if you'd like to discuss some work, I'm more than willing to listen."

Shiv nods, then taps a file that is lying on the right side of his table. I pick up the file. It's the employment agreement. After a quick scan, I sign it and push the file back towards him.

Shiv looks disinterested. Then points to a stack of files lying on left side of his table. These are files of pending projects. "The client hasn't agreed to the interior designs we've presented so far. I'm sure you can come up with designs that the client likes so that we can go ahead with these projects."

I pick up the files and look at them. There are about 14 of them. I nod.

It will take me months to study and understand what went wrong the last time round and why clients rejected the designs that Variety had presented to them.

Then I will have to understand specific client requirements and then finally present them with alternate designs customised to their needs. Shiv is drowning me in work. That's his game plan. Keep her busy and overwhelmed with work so that he can keep an eye on me. So, what is he doing behind my back?

Shiv looks at me irritated. "Is there anything you want to ask?"

"No. I was wondering how much time do I have to finish all these projects."

"I want them done immediately. So, make it fast. And keep me updated on your progress every week."

"Alright."

"Alright Sir! You will address me as Sir from henceforth."

"Yes Sir."

Shiv goes back to looking at his laptop signalling the end of the meeting. I walk out holding 14 bulky files. As I'm walking back to my table, I notice everyone looking at me and grinning.

Sarah the brunette comes close to me and says softly, "The last interior designer was fired over these same projects. So, you better crack them quickly. Best of luck." She disappears back into the crowd looking at me as I finally reach my station and dump the files on my desk.

I wasn't expecting my work life in Variety to be easy. Shiv just made sure that it would be miserable. I swear to myself that I will reciprocate in kind and make Shiv's life even more miserable at the first given opportunity.

As I start pouring through the files, a thought gently eases itself into my head – Shiv Patel's office is eerie because it's perfect. Perfect for him! There's nothing unnecessary in it. No one book, not one painting, not one chair. No item in his office is stuff that he didn't want or need. Everything in it is either what he needs to run his office or what he wants the world to see. This means that he's a perfectionist, an absolute control freak and would hate things not being exactly the way he wanted. I smile to myself knowing that I've found something that was useful to me.

"Hmm, looks like someone's already started work and didn't even notice me or say hello!"

I freeze in my seat – the same dreamy voice and so close to me. I look up and smile as Neil stands looking like a Greek God.

Tall, wearing a light blue well ironed, fitted shirt showing his bulging abs, hip hugging dark blue pants and well-polished black shoes, and that cologne of his which makes me want to rip every piece of cloth on him and take every ounce of him in me. He clears his throat as he leans forward with an I-know-what-you're-thinking-smile on his face as I quickly close the tote, grab my bag and proceed towards the office café to get away from him before I do anything stupid in front of everyone on my first day. I rely on sarcasm to get me through my muddled head space.

"Yes, your dad welcomed me with these 14 projects on my

very first day. I suppose this is what you guys call training in this company."

Neil laughs.

"He's challenging you. If you ace this challenge and retain all 14 clients, you'll become employee of the month and get promoted to permanent employee really quickly. That's what you want right?"

I don't like these mixed feelings that I get when I'm with Neil. I'm irritated at his enthusiasm but just can't seem to express it. I need to get away from him, the closer I stay to him, the harder it is for me to control my thoughts about him and that could lead to something I really don't want right now.

"Hmm...?" Neil prompts me to reply to his question.

I can't. My mind is filled with all the things I want to do with him. I go into the washroom feeling flushed.

You are here for a purpose – don't forget that. Use him as a pawn and nothing more, play hard to get so that he comes after you and not the other way around. So, get out there, do what you're here for and focus. I auto suggest as I look in the mirror while washing my hands before heading out into my battle ground – it's time to get to work.

I SPEND the next month slaving away day and night. I take my files home and work at all hours, often calling clients directly to figure out what they want.

Neil keeps making an appearance whenever I'm in office. It's like the Devil is making available exclusively to me the most delicious affectionate handsome man as my biggest temptation and I'm forced to say no. He tries to come home but I don't allow him to meet me anywhere outside office.

I sense his growing restlessness and I ignore it only to find out that he's even more desperate to meet me the next time around. Carol helps me by focusing on her secret project and not allowing me to start a new conversation. Even when I want to talk to her and ask her about her exciting hacking projects, she tells me that she's busy and forces me to focus on my work.

Over time, my resolve to stick to completing the tremendous amount of work grows until I'm obsessed with completing all fourteen projects within a month.

There are days when going to office becomes meaningless so I just stay at home and work. I try and use every minute of my time to somehow complete my workload for the day.

With Carol making sure that I eat well and plying me with endless coffees, I'm able to manage a humongous amount of work on most days. I make it a point to email Shiv and update him on a regular basis.

AFTER A MONTH, when I've finished all fourteen projects and proven my worth to the company, Carol celebrates by spiking my drink. I'm knocked out unconscious for eighteen hours. After that she forces me to take two days off and feeds me with the best food she can think of.

After two days of complete rest I emerge fully recharged and rejoin work at the office. I make it a point to email Neil and let him know that no interior designer in Variety had achieved so much in such little time.

Neil is amazed at me and my accomplishment. He invites me to drinks and dinner for the seventh time in a month. I realise that I'm fighting my own self. I can no longer resist the intense love and affection I'm receiving from Neil and keep saying no to him especially when I secretly crave for every bit of attention I get from him. It seems cruel to do this to an obviously decent and innocent soul. I should either clearly tell him that I'm not interested or go with the flow and let things happen between us. Keeping him hanging is becoming unbearable even for me so I level with the only person in the world I can trust who I have been inadvertently ignoring for the last one month.

"I've completed a month in Variety and I can say for sure it's not been a smooth ride. Shiv has tried everything possible to make my life a living hell in that company and I, on my part, have successfully faced every tough situation created for me, emerged stronger than I give credit to myself for." I pick on my food as Carol looks at me intently – I've never been this confused or unsure about anything before.

"As hard as it has been, I've been successful in dodging Neil's advances and dinner proposals, but if I continue doing it, I'll be betraying a core value that I've held on to all my life – never hurt the innocent. Also, he'll suspect that I've played him and used him to get into the company and that could ruin our plan. I desperately want him, want to be with him and at the same time I don't want to respond to his proposals – it's like I'm in a 'Catch-22' situation"

Carol smiles as if she knew the situation I was in. We've been best friends and sisters for the last fifteen years and she knows me better than anyone ever could. She leans forward and takes my hands in hers and says something that I've avoided for so long, "You have developed intense feelings for him and it's hard for you to keep a check on your feelings, am I right?"

I nod in agreement as tears roll down my eyes – for the first time I feel lost and vulnerable instead of strong and confident; guess that's what love does to you!!

"This was not supposed to happen and now I don't know how to stop it," I wipe my tears.

Carol sits back and racks her chair waiting for me to look up and have a meaningful conversation with her.

After a couple of minutes, I look up and find her staring at me, waiting for me. She again leans forward, pushes her plate away and places her elbows on the table as she speaks in a motherly tone, "Hun, you need to keep your distance and concentrate on your goal. If you allow Neil Patel to confuse you, you will not achieve what you've set out to achieve. Neil Patel is a playboy. He's been with more women that I can keep track of. He's had flings and one night stands with girls all over Vancouver. This is just an infatuation for him and if you keep resisting him, eventually he will get the message and back off. If you don't resist him and give in to him, you will have a wonderful six months and then he'll dump you and move on to swearing undying love to the next pretty thing he sees. You know all of this!"

"Yeah I do but..."

"And as far as your goal of destroying Shiv Patel is concerned, you will fail miserably and probably end up either in a jail or maybe even dead; because Shiv is not ordinary enemy to have. I was talking to Kevin Mathews about Shiv the other day and he told me that Shiv has been investigated in the past as well. The police suspected him of wrong doing when his mistress died. But they couldn't prove anything and he paid big sums of money to get out of trouble."

I sip on my wine and twirl the spaghetti with the fork, deciding if I want to eat or talk or maybe do both. She taps her fingers on the table to get my attention and gives me a 'do-you-understand' look. I decide to vent it all out.

"But I'm confused because I know that the connection with Neil is real. I feel it. And I know that he feels it. It's like I'm just postponing the inevitable and it's getting really hard."

Carol keeps looking at me waiting for me to finish. I drink some more wine as I continue, "It doesn't seem fair that I should break Neil's heart because of what his father has done. Yes, Shiv Patel is a monster who destroyed my life and took my parents away from me, but how does it make sense to make Neil suffer for his father's mistakes. How does that make me different from Shiv? Shiv went about building his empire using whatever means available to him and when the accident he caused, killed my parents, he covered it up and tried everything he could to break me so that I would never rise up and challenge him. He was merely eliminating what he thought could be a potential problem. My life was just collateral damage – a casualty of war. I don't want to be like that. I don't want Neil to suffer because of his father's sins."

Carol holds my hand again as she calmly and quietly listening to me venting out my inner confusion.

"Can you really manage both at the same time Nal? Ask yourself that question! Can you really manage to destroy Shiv and reciprocate Neil's love back to him? Do you really see a future with Neil after you're done destroying his father?!"

Finally, the penny drops in my head. Carol is right. Even if I naively imagine it to be possible, I know for a fact that Neil will dump me the moment he finds out my designs on his father. I have to choose one or the other. Either I pursue a relationship with Neil or I go about taking my revenge. Both are not possible simultaneously. This is what sisters are for. Thank God for Carol.

"Look, I know this isn't as easy as it seems, but we both know how strong and determined you are. Now I want you to put this dreamy, 'I-am-so-in-love' girl to sleep and awaken that feisty, strong, independent girl who wants to avenge the death of her parents and the seven years of complete humiliation and endless abuse that you suffered because of that monster Shiv Patel." I nod as I try to hold back my tears. We strategise on how I should work to get what I've gone there for. Carol notices me looking lost. We finish the rest of the dinner in silence, not wanting to discuss anymore as it got very taxing and emotionally draining.

I LOOK around at the dozens of partygoers dancing their worries away, as Carol drags me into the 'Just Kiss, Don't Tell' Club that is thriving with music. I struggle to hear what she's saying over the loud music. She finally takes me to the center of the dance floor and shouts into my ears.

"Do you know why I've brought you here?" I shrug my shoulders with an I-don't-know-why expression.

"I want you to try and pick any guy you like!"

I look at her surprised. Carol hates going into crowded public places and does it only when she absolutely has to and yet here we

WHAT COMES FROM WITHIN

are. I figure out that she's trying to help me clear my head. She moves my head around forcing me to look at four or five handsome stags in a corner waiting for an opportunity to introduce themselves. She gives me a what-do-you-think expression and then without waiting for my answer, she grabs my hand and takes me towards the young men.

"I'm not sure I want to do this." I tell her.

"I know. Think of this as a test. If you can hook up with any guy you like, then you're not in love with Neil. But if you can't, then you know what you have to do."

As we reach the young men, she looks at them and smiles. "My friend here is going through a bad time. Her name is Nalini Shah."

One young guy introduces himself but the music is too loud for me to hear his name clearly. He holds my hand and walks me towards the center of the dance floor. As we begin dancing, we exchange a few smiles. I look back at Carol who winks at me. The man although very polite puts his arm around me and tells me to go with the flow of the music. I see Carol has also picked up another guy and they've begun dancing close-by. I decide to listen to her advice and let go of my inhibitions. We enjoy dancing and drinking for the next hour by which time I'm really exhausted and drunk.

We sit down in the lounge area nearby and continue with our drinks and conversation. I realise how messed up I really am when I'm unable to pay attention to him. I keep thinking of Neil and what he would think if he were here in the club. The man keeps talking about himself and what he's doing and I keep nodding politely until he comes close to kissing me. Just then, as if involuntarily I push him away. He mumbles something that looks like pleading with me for a kiss but I'm unable to pay any attention to him.

As he gently holds me and moves closer to my face for a kiss, I push him away and walk out of the club. Carol notices me leaving through the exit door and comes rushing after me along with the man. By the time Carol makes her way out of the crowded club, I'm already on my way home in a cab. Carol shakes her head.

The man asks her what he'd done wrong. Carol tells him to forget about me; that I'm in love with someone else and can't take my mind off him. The man shrugs his shoulders and goes back into the club.

EVEN BEFORE I step out of the elevator on the 23rd floor, I find Neil waiting for me. As the others in the elevator leave, Neil walks in and nudges me back inside – we are alone and I can hear my heart thumping against my chest, butterflies in my tummy and face hot and blushing. He presses the button to temporarily stop the elevator and then gently places his hand on my back and pulls me close to him, making my heart skip a beat.

I try hard to not get affected by him but my mind and body are simply overwhelmed with emotion the moment he comes close to me. And he is close, too close! I can smell his musk cologne and it makes me want to grab him and...

"I hope you like cappuccino and chocolate cheese cake." He whispers in my ear while tucking a strand of my hair behind my ear.

"Neil, I, umm, I have to start my shift, please. I've had my breakfast – maybe on the weekend, my treat." I try to talk my way out of this, as I feel rushed.

He smiles, pulls me even closer and I feel him hard against me – releases the elevator and pushes M for main floor – all the while holding me and looking me in the eye.

He holds my hand and takes me to the nearby café. I follow him like a lost puppy, not making any effort to leave his hand.

"I am super proud of you and what you've achieved in the last one month. Consider this my way of saying thank you for living up to the faith I showed in you. I fought with my dad to get you this job and today my dad has nothing to say to me about you. That just shows what you've achieved."

WE SIT across from each other, trying to make small talk while we wait for our coffees, chocolate and blueberry cheesecakes. I feel it once again, an irresistible pull towards him without him even touching me. I can see in his eyes that he feels the same towards me. The difference between us is that he has given in to it and I haven't. Since ignoring him isn't possible, I decide to go with the next best option and flirt with him. Neil reciprocates and we're really into each other. When I'm with him it's almost as if our bodies are talking to each other – our hands, our eyes, our legs. He finally asks me to go on a weekend date with him and I promise him that I'll think about it and let him know soon.

"Ms. SHAH, please come to my office." Shiv Patel's voice booms on the office speaker as Neil and I enter after our little coffee date. I let go of his hand and run to my desk to hurriedly collect the paperwork spread on my desk and with a note pad and rush to his office for a meeting. I enter his office to find a few other people sitting having a meeting.

"Come in Ms. Shah, have a seat." He does not look up and continues to work on a file. I hesitantly walk in quite aware of glaring, judging looks; I must admit, I feel very uncomfortable. Fortunately, I find a corner seat and hope that I am well hidden.

"So, now that we have everyone here, let's start the meeting." Shiv Patel gets up and walk across the room towards a white board.

AFTER AN HOUR, we are asked to make an action plan and present it in a couple weeks and the meeting is adjourned.

"Ms. Shah, please stay back. I need to talk to you."

My heart is pounding and suddenly my mouth is dry. I sit across from him and wait for him to finish his conversation. He clears his throat as he closes the door and sits across from me, a grim look on his face.

"Ms. Shah, I don't like to beat around the bush and will come straight to the point; you're doing well as an employee but keep it limited to that. Keep your distance from Neil. I don't know what your motive is, but be assured that I will not let you play any games with my son. I hired you because Neil insisted on it, not because I wanted to and let me make it very clear: you are not and will never be suitable for Neil. You're here to work for us, so don't try any tricks here, remember I'm always watching you."

I look him in the eye and with every bit of confidence in me say, "looks like you have a lot of misconceptions Mr. Patel – about yourself and your wealth; but one thing I can assure you, I am here to make my career and I know what I need to do for that. I have already proved myself with your existing clients. Instead of keeping an eye on me, why don't you keep an eye on your son." Before he can respond I pick up my stuff and walk out.

"NALINI, I WANT THIS REPORT..." Neil suddenly walks up to my desk and sees me glaring furiously at the computer screen while absent-mindedly scribbling on a piece of paper. He gently places his hand on my shoulder startling me, "hey, you ok? All well? What happened in there?"

Neil comes and sits on my desk facing me – a concerned look on his face; I look up, lean back in my chair and cross my legs before sarcastically saying, "why don't you go ask your father – the man thinks I'm here, not as an interior designer but because I want to seduce you and use you to make it big in the company. I hope he is wrong about your reasons for hiring me because if he is not, I swear I will not forgive you ever."

He sighs, puts a file on my desk, leans forward and says, "I'll talk to him – don't worry, everyone knows how good you are.

Trust me, I will sort everything out – you just concentrate on your job, start working on this file ASAP." He pats me on my shoulder and walks towards Shiv's office.

"Shiv Patel, you want to play games with me, sure let's play! I will answer all your questions but through your son. In no time, you will be forced to agree to all my terms – just wait and watch, the games have just begun." I swirl in my chair smiling as I see Neil pace in Shiv's room arguing with him before working on the file he left on my desk.

PART of my plan in Variety over the last month has been to get familiar with all the key people especially the staff that manages the office. I buy presents for everyone – the janitors, the cleaners, the maintenance staff, the clerical and IT staff and all my co-workers in Variety.

I take notes on their birthdays and anniversaries and present them with gifts appropriate for each one of them. I discreetly lend money to quite a few of the support staff to help them tide over their financial problems.

My goal is to get staff in the company to like and appreciate me. This move yields results quickly and I gain access to some really important and confidential files including company expense reports. At lunchtime, when most of the staff leaves for an hour, I stick around and sneak into the photocopy room to make copies of the expense reports.

Shiv and his company have faked expenses every year in multiple client accounts and paid out money to their own shell companies to avoid paying taxes. Over the years they have accumulated hundreds of thousands of dollars in their shell companies that do very little work but charge Variety substantial amounts. I'm quite nervous doing all this out in the open but I have over the years learnt to control my nerves with meditation. I cautiously make copies, keeping an eye for anyone coming in.

"How do I have the pleasure of your company in the copier room?"

I take a deep breath and turn around and see Neil leaning against the door in his tight shirt and hip hugging trousers; if I wasn't in the office, I would have ripped his clothes off, wrapped my legs around him and pushed him all the way in. I feel sweat trickling from my forehead and I smile back, "Well, what are the odds. What are you doing here – it's lunch time, shouldn't you be out having lunch with your father?"

He comes inside and closes the door behind him, "I thought of having a little quality time with you, after all, we both know there is something between us which hasn't been named yet."

I tense up as he comes close, takes me in his arms and whispers, "what I would do to have this one kiss from you?"

I pull back, put my hand on his lips and drop a gentle kiss, "there, happy now?"

He looks amused and tries to kiss me again and as much as I want it, I control myself and say, "Easy tiger, we're in the work place and this is not work appropriate. Why don't I take a rain check and we can start the fire when we go out for dinner on the weekend."

He smiles, kisses me on the cheek. I heave a sigh of relief as Neil leaves the room. That was a narrow escape. If Neil was anything like his father, he would have found out what I was photocopying and got me arrested. Now as punishment for being found alone in the photocopy room, I will have to go out for dinner with him because if I don't, he will start questioning every assumption he's made about me, including whether I'm trustworthy or not and what I was doing in the copier room.

THE PROBLEM with having a man fall intensely in love with you is that they often end up taking an all-or-nothing approach with you. Either you completely belong to them, or you get kicked out of their life and become nothing to them. I have to pace this relationship to my convenience. I collect the copies that I made and rush out before anyone else comes in.

TWO HOURS LATER, the security staff install cameras both inside and outside the copier room. Obviously, the security team is monitoring me all the time on Shiv's instructions and they have informed Shiv about Neil and me meeting up in the photocopy room. So, Shiv is suspicious about what I was doing in there and wants to keep an eye on what I do in the office. Damn! No more photocopying for me except for officially sanctioned documents. Another door closes.

WITHIN MINUTES of the cameras getting installed, I get called to the security room where the head of security asks me to sit. As I sit in front of him, my heart is pounding away and I struggle to control my nervousness. I can feel the sweat in my armpits. The security in-charge who has obviously been instructed by Shiv asks me what I was photocopying in the photocopy room. I give him an evasive answer.

I was making copies of the designs I'd already made for the 14 projects I was working on so that I could file them and use them as reference for future projects. The head-of-security smiles as he informs me that the company didn't allow employees, especially interns to keep any copies of their work with themselves. That if I ever wanted to refer to projects already completed, I could use the official online database created at Variety after obtaining permission from the boss.

AS I APOLOGISE for my mistake, one security guard brings my handbag, files and all my other stuff into the room. He looks at me and then at the head-of-security. The head of security opens the bag and empties out all its contents onto the table. As he searches through my stuff and then the bag, my anxiety reaches an all-time high. I know that if I object to this unannounced search, it will raise suspicion so I just smile at him.

THE HEAD of security is surprised at not finding anything incriminating. He looks at my files and sees the photocopies that I've made. He keeps all my design files with himself. I try to control my nerves and pretend as if I didn't care about being searched without consent. Soon the search is done and he asks me to gather all my stuff and go back to my desk. I quickly put all my stuff back and walk out. That was a really close call. The security guard didn't look into the trash can near my desk where I had thrown all the shredded photocopies. He also didn't notice the accounts admin staff quietly picking up from my desk, the file I'd sneaked out of the accounts room.

What I'm relieved about most of all is that they didn't bother checking the photos on my phone because they would have found photos of all the documents I wasn't supposed to have access to. That was a close call and never to be done again.

It's best to tell the staff to take photos themselves and upload it to my online cloud storage from their homes.

Shiv Patel is obviously on to me and must be watching me. I casually look around in the room to find a security camera pointed directly at me. As I get back to my desk, I find a note from Shiv asking me to prepare custom designs and costing for a list of 38 prospective clients to who we're trying to sell our latest commercial office property.

SHIV PATEL WINS this round and has now got all eyes fixed on me. I immediately call my new friend the janitor to empty out the trash can I'd used an hour ago just to make sure that no one gets any smart ideas later on.

Chapter Seven

I feel like a convicted criminal waiting for the proverbial axe to fall on me and sever my head.

Shiv monitors every movement I make in office and I start noticing cameras everywhere I go.

It's like being in a jail except that I chose to be here. I take it easy and limit myself only to office work with the occasional short casual chat with office employees.

Shiv has ensured that I can't do anything else in the office and for the next few days, I give in and don't even try to snoop around hoping that after surveilling me for a few days he would lose interest in my boring office life.

I tell Carol about what's going on and she's immediately suspicious. She gets us new laptops and phones and tells me to control my online footprint, so I stick to the usual websites and apps.

We also decide not to say anything suspicious on the phone so that even if Shiv has got his spies listening in to our calls, they won't hear anything alarming.

Being constantly aware of what I'm doing and not having the freedom to live the way I want takes its toll on me and I'm dying to break out of this self-inflicted prison as soon as I can.

Carol just laughs off all my worries and tells me that she's been living in a prison-like-state ever since she started taking up confidential hacking jobs through her anonymous online sources. I think about her life since the age of 13 and see how careful she is with everything. She mostly stays at home and never goes out unless she absolutely has to. She changes all her gadgets, devices and phone number every year and never stays in the same area for more than two years. She hides behind many different anonymous online identities and erases any identity that she feels might be under the scanner.

Also, if she has to download anything remotely suspicious, she hacks someone else's Wi-Fi to do it so that she can protect herself. It's a tough life, but the amount of money she earns more than makes up for it.

Thinking about her life gives me the strength to carry on and I pledge to never complain again.

Then one day, we relax our guard and our illusion about living a secure protected life gets shattered. My college mate from the US, Susan Allen calls me up and asks the both of us to meet her. The joy of meeting a long-lost friend compels us to go meet her. We leave the house in a rush and drive off to meet her.

ADRIAN WAITS for a long time after Nal and Carol have left their apartment building. Once he's sure that they are not fooling him, he walks into the apartment building with a quiet confidence.

As he reaches their floor, he pauses and looks around to see if there are any security cameras to spot him. He doesn't find any, so he goes to the door and uses a master key and a metal wire to snap it open. Then he slowly enters the apartment to check whether there are any security cameras inside. Once he's sure that the hacker girl had not put any such security systems in place, he walks in and closes the door behind him. He walks through the entire apartment checking every room and space to make sure that there is no one inside. After making sure that it's absolutely safe for him to go about his work, he starts working quietly.

First, he photographs the entire apartment, then goes about clicking photographs of everything of relevance to the job he'd been given. He clicks photos of the computers and laptops, how many electronic devices they had left in the house, what kind of books they read, what food they kept inside their refrigerator, what kind of documents or identification they had. He opens up a stack of letters and bank-statements and clicks photos of each one of them – everything that could be useful to him later on. He works at a brisk pace and finishes finding out everything he can about them.

Every now and then he's surprised by what he sees but doesn't waste any time in trying to think. Finally, he leaves behind a token of his presence on Nalini's laptop and walks out of the apartment within eleven minutes of entering it.

SUSAN HAS a strange way of holding a conversation. All three of us meet up at a wonderful place called "My Alibi" and we notice that while reminiscing about the old times, she speaks about our lives as if she's memorised it from a text book.

While both Carol and I were nursing our drinks over a few shared memories, Susan keeps looking around as if fearful of something or someone. Both Carol and I know that something's going on and wait for her to open up. An hour and a half later, after the third vodka, Susan asks us a strange question; whether we had been doing anything suspicious.

Carol is taken aback by the question because no one except me knows what she's up to and everything about her secret hacker life is hidden very well from the world.

I notice the frown lines on Carol's face and decide to take charge of the conversation. I ask Susan what she meant and inform her that the only change in our lives was me getting a job at a real estate firm. Susan looks surprised as if she's trying to figure something out. She then asks me if I was up to something that might get attention from the authorities. I confidently tell her that I'm only an overworked interior designer working for a boss who doesn't like me too much.

Susan appears even more surprised and looks at us strangely as if we didn't fit into her preconceived ideas about what we would tell her so I decide to confront her and ask her a direct question.

"What are you trying to tell us Susan?"

"There's someone inquiring about the both of you. Someone is going around asking a lot of questions about the both of you, especially about you, Nalini. I got a call asking me about my relationship with you, who you dated, where you lived. The questions went on and on. I just thought that I should inform you that someone's doing a thorough check on you guys. I hope everything's okay."

Carol makes light of the incident and brushes it off as a background check being done by my paranoid employers.

Susan looks confused. "I've been background checked by my employers but this is way beyond just checking for a person's suitability for a job. This was asking personal stuff and trying to find out secrets. When I got uncomfortable, I decided to end the call and since then I've been getting the feeling that I'm being followed."

Both of us laugh it off and tell her that she's being paranoid. That she had nothing to worry about and that we didn't care about any background check. We ask her for the number that has been calling her, so that we can look into it and Susan gladly shares that number with us. She then asks us if she can call us in case there is a problem. She holds my hand and tells me that she's worried about herself and that if her fiancé's family found out about her talking to strangers who were snooping around into her past then they might end her engagement.

I keep listening to Susan and wonder whether she's worried

about us or herself. What is it that she really wanted? She used to be a fun person as a student and would hang out with us and even go to the beach every month but now she appears to be a completely different person. We tell her not to worry and ask her to call us if there is a problem.

Just then Carol gets a message on her Signal App. She immediately informs us that she needed to leave for a work-related matter. I tell her to go ahead and that I'll come back home in a cab later on. I stay back because I want to pry out some more information from Susan.

CAROL IS in the Jim Horton's café struggling to connect to a high-speed Wi-Fi completely unaware that a man is clicking her photographs from his car outside the café. She looks around then decides to scan all the Wi-Fis in the range of her laptop and finally finds one that has a strong connection. She then goes about getting its password using a hacker app on her laptop. Within a few minutes, she's in.

She smiles to herself at her minor accomplishment, completely unaware that an intense looking man in a black hat and long overcoat is looking around in her car. As she chats with her hacker network over what seems like a harmless online gaming site, the man quickly looks about in the car, clicks photos of all the documents, then shuts the car and leaves as if he were a ghost.

Carol who is completely unaware of the man, tries to concentrate on her work but there's too much anxiety going around. Her hacker network is super excited about completing their pet project that they believed would completely change the world.

"The Nutcracker" as they liked to call the project had kept them busy for years. They knew the secrets of some large corporations and were appalled by the amount of power and influence a small number of billionaires had over how things were being run. Sworn to set things right and expose the misdeeds of the powerful elite, they had hacked their way into exposing the secrets and wrong doings of billion-dollar corporations that were destroying the environment, manipulating people, destabilising countries and even managing human trafficking networks that had devastated the lives of millions of young girls from across the world.

However, things didn't seem to make the kind of impact that they had wanted. This had frustrated them over the years and they yearned for irrefutable evidence of the wrong doings and atrocities that were being committed across the world. They had as a side project decided to create their own hacking software that could work on any phone or device – spyware that would grant them the evidence they needed to expose the powers behind the endless suffering being inflicted upon people.

Today was the day they had succeeded and were going live on their secret website.

Carol waits anxiously for the "The Nutcracker" to go live. She checks her laptop yet again for the seventeenth time in the less than the twenty minutes that she was in the café. It was time for her to leave now. It wasn't safe for her to be connected to some random Wi-Fi for more than twenty minutes.

Just as she's about to leave, she clears her browsing history and checks the secret website one more time. It's live!

The most intrusive surveillance software in the world was live and available to a select group of hackers who had helped develop it. Carol was one of those chosen few! She quickly logs in with her username and password and she's in! She downloads the software onto her computer and then starts uploading it onto her personal secret website. It's done within ten minutes. She could now do a lot of hacking and surveilling on her own and help bring down evil monsters like Shiv Patel easily.

"Finally!" she unconsciously screams out!

Everyone in the café looks at her wondering what happened. Carol mumbles a quiet apology, then quickly shuts down her computer and leaves the café.

As soon as she gets to her car, she pushes the door unlock

button on the car key but it doesn't respond. She presses it one more time and the car doors get locked. Carol is immediately alarmed. This means just one thing, someone was inside her car. She unlocks the car and looks inside.

Everything seemed to be in place so nothing was stolen. Obviously, someone was spying on her. She quickly looks through all the car documents and sees that someone had rummaged through them very quickly and had forgotten to put everything back in the exact order that she usually kept all her stuff. This clearly meant one of two things – either someone in her hacker group had hacked her and leaked her identity. But wait! The hacker group was completely confidential and no details of any hacker could be accessed by anyone. The hacker network was designed to function completely anonymously. Nothing except a fake online identity could be found out. Which then meant that the other option was true - Shiv Patel had unleashed his dogs on Nalini and she was caught in the crossfire. Neither scenario seemed either safe to her. She gets into her car and drives back home at top speed.

CAROL CAUTIOUSLY ENTERS OUR APARTMENT. Everything is exactly as it is. Nothing seems to have been touched. She immediately calls me up. I'm still sitting with Susan Allen and we've finished off a bottle of vodka between us. Both of us are totally drunk and laughing at the silliest of things.

I try and pry information out of Susan who seems to have made up her mind not to give out any more. I did learn though that Susan Allen's name was Susan Wong and that she'd discarded her father's name and taken up her stepfather's surname to blend in. Both of us decide to call it a night and we head out in different directions.

I'm so drunk that I don't notice the 28 missed calls from Carol. As I finally reach the entrance, I'm blinded by the bright glaring lights against a dark sky.

I must have been in 'My Alibi' for over 4 hours! I take out my phone to call a cab when I notice Carol rushing in. I'm barely sober and crash into Carol's arms the moment I see her. Carol looks relieved that she's finally found me and hugs me with more emotion than she's ever displayed in public during the course of her adult life.

ADRIAN GETS OUT of a taxi and walks into a dimly lit parking lot located in the basement of an old building. It's well past 2 at night and pitch dark. He struggles to look around and doesn't see anyone except an opulent sedan parked with its engine turned on. He recognises the car immediately and quietly goes and sits in the car. Then turns around and looks at Shiv as he shows the photos to him.

Shiv looks at the current photos of Nalini and Carol and compares them to the photos of Nisha and Emma. "It's the same two girls. How they created new identities for themselves after faking their deaths, still remains a mystery to me. But it is the two of them for sure. Now find holes in their fake identities. There must be something or someone that helped them, do whatever you have to but bring me proof and I'll blow this wide open. I'll put the both of them in jail and make sure they never bother me or my son again."

Adrian keeps staring at Shiv. Shiv looks back at Adrian and they both know what Adrian must do. Shiv nods and Adrian leaves the car.

I WAKE up to the relentless buzzing of my cell phone that is getting charged. My head is throbbing, I feel dizzy and my lips are parched, "told you, don't drink so much; but do you ever listen?"

I look around to find that we're in some new place. Before I can make sense of what is happening, Carol pushes a huge glass of lemon water towards me. She pulls me up and makes me sit up right, "not a word, shut up and drink this." She shoves the glass in my hand, picks up my phone and takes the call; "Hi, this is Carol. Nal is not feeling well today, I'll ask her to call you when she wakes up." Click. Before I can utter a word, she hangs up and throws the phone on the bed.

"Oh, by the way that was Neil Patel on the phone asking why you didn't show up at work today" she casually remarks and walks out without looking at me. I sit alone trying to figure out what's going on.

"Where are we?" I ask meekly.

"We're in the Blue Horizon Hotel. Breakfast will be ready in half an hour, I suggest you shower, call Neil and take a day off. A lot has happened that you need to be updated on. So, get cracking."

I drink the lemon water and leave a voice message on Neil's phone excusing myself from coming to work for the day. I inform him that the work he had given me would be completed and handed over to him tomorrow.

I feel better after having informed Neil, now it's time to find out what Carol was up to. I quickly drink up a strong coffee, a bottle full of water and swallow an Advil just to come back to my senses. Then I somehow manage to shower and finally an hour later show up in front of Carol who gestures to me to keep quiet.

Carol puts on loud music on her phone, then switches off the electricity in the room using the hotel room key card switch, hands me a cup of coffee, makes me sit on a chair and breathe deeply as she rushes to get her laptop.

"What's going on?" I ask. "Why are you being paranoid? Is there someone listening to us?"

"I'm just being cautious. And yes, someone's spying on us. Someone looked through my car yesterday. Don't you remember even Susan told us yesterday about someone prying into our backgrounds? They went to our apartment and left this photo."

I look at the photo and my face turns red. It's a photo of

Carol and me when we were about 12 years old. Both of us are looking outside our window and our faces are clearly visible.

"How's this possible? I thought we had taken away all the photos lying with Jack." I'm still not functioning at a 100%.

"We did. This photo isn't from Jack's collection of photos."

My face goes red. "Oh my God! It's Shiv's guy who was snooping on us?!"

Carol smiles. "Yes! He obviously knows that we're Emma and Nisha. That's why he left the photo. He knows and this means Shiv knows our real identities. Now they'll try and find holes in the fake story we've created along with our new identities. We need to find out what they know. We need to act before they do."

"How? I don't know what they're up to!"

Carol smiles. "But we now have the means to find out."

I look at Carol puzzled.

"Do you remember Project Nutcracker?!"

"Yes. The hacking software for phones and laptops. I thought you guys couldn't do it and had given up on that?!"

"No. That's the story we told everyone. But we kept working. We just got more people to join us. More than eight hundred anonymous programmers spent six years building it as a joint project. It's done. I've got it!"

She looks at me staring at her clueless, then pulls her chair next to me and runs me through the new software on her laptop.

"This, once downloaded on a computer, a tablet or a phone becomes a virtual door into their system. All their contacts, photos, files, apps. Everything! I can virtually clone anyone's phone if this software is installed on their phone."

My eyes open wide as I understand the implications of this. Carol continues trying to simplify everything for my benefit.

"This software once downloaded into a phone, turns their phone into a listening device enabling me to listen to all their conversations and record them."

I'm kind of overwhelmed just knowing how advanced hacking has become. I still remember that I had to physically sneak into Variety and copy the files from Shiv's computer using a thumb drive just a few weeks ago.

Carol pulls my hand to make me concentrate on what she's saying, "You do know that most modern devices store their data in the cloud." I nod.

"This is just like that. Once this software is downloaded into any device, it mimics the cloud and stores all the information from the device into the cloud. The difference is, this cloud is controlled by us. It's like their computer uses their Wi-Fi to back up everything to our cloud giving us the access to all their files."

My head is now pounding as the information being given is a lot for me to comprehend and understand under the given circumstances.

"One thing I've not been able to understand – why would someone want to download this 'spyware' on their computers and cell phones?"

Carol leans forward and looking intently at me and says, "No one will knowingly download it – they will have to be tricked into downloading it. Like when people knowingly download a cool new free app from an unknown company just because it looks like a cool fun game or whatever. This functions in the exact same way. We just insert the software onto their device one way or another. Once downloaded, it does the job on its own. No further action is required."

"And what if the person we want to hack, doesn't download this app? Then what?"

Carol looks pleased that I'm beginning to understand what's going on. "In that case, we have to gain access to their device, go to my secret website using their web browser and click on download software button. That's it!"

"So, you want to steal their phone and then download the software?"

Carol is happy that I've finally got it! Exclaims "Yes!"

I understand what Carol is trying to say to me. She wants me to access Shiv and Neil's devices, their phones and laptops. Both of us look at each other.

Carol puts her hand on my shoulder. "You do this and you will always know what Patel Senior and Junior are up to. You will always be one step ahead of them."

My brain is still not working at full capacity. "But..."

Carol holds my face. You've already got Neil all excited about your weekend date, right?!

"Yes."

Carol breaks it down into simple seemingly easy steps for me. "You will have to seduce Neil or maybe even spend a night with him and then, once he's sound asleep, download the software on his device."

"But how will I manage gaining access to Shiv's devices?"

We ponder over some ideas and then come up with a plan, which is risky but the only way to get this done. I open up my laptop and show a draft email that I'd composed several weeks ago to Carol. Carol looks worried but I reassure her that we needed to fight back else we'd lose the war to Shiv. Carol finally nods. I quickly hit the send button. Within minutes a gossip columnist in India gets an anonymous email.

"Done! Let Shiv Patel deal with this. I'm not going to get intimidated by him."

Carol looks worried as I start detailing out all the things we need to do before we head back into our apartment.

The next morning, I reach the office two hours before my shift. I'm glad that I'm the first to come to the office. I'm aware of the security cameras covering ever step I take and follow me around the office. I pick up the file that Neil gave me and then calmly create an alibi as planned and call Neil.

"Hi Neil, sorry to bother you at this hour – I actually came early today to cover up for yesterday and was working on the file that you gave me, but I need some documents from Mr. Patel's cabin. Would it be okay for me to go in there and get them please?"

A sleepy Neil answers my call with a simple, "Yeah yeah, go ahead, do what you want but please don't wake me up this early." I smile as I disconnect the call after recording it – to be on the safe side.

I enter Shiv Patel's room knowing fully well that I need to work really fast. I open Shiv Patel's computer, start it up and much to my surprise, he still hasn't installed a login password. I open the web browser, go to Carol's secret website and start downloading the software into his laptop while keeping an eye on anyone coming in. As the software is downloading, I gather the documents necessary to show the security cameras that I'm carrying additional documents out of Shiv's office with me after having spoken to Neil about it.

"Hi Miss Shah, if you're done with your work, can I clean the office?"

The janitor's voice startles me. I recognise her as the Asian woman whose mother had contracted Covid and then had to borrow a lot of money to keep her family going. I had helped her out financially and she recognises me.

"Hi Lisa, yes, I'm almost done."

I calm my nerves and pretend to go about business as if I'm doing only what is required and expected of me. I go back up to Shiv's laptop to check. The download is complete. I shut the window, clean up the browsing history. Then shut down the laptop while continuing the conversation with her.

"How's your mother doing?"

"She's is well. And thanks to you I was able to keep her comfortable."

"You're always welcome Lisa. Any help you need, just tell me."

"Thank you, Miss Shah."

I calmly collect my stuff and walk back to my desk.

As soon as I reach my desk, I call Carol. "It's done!"

Carol starts checking things out on her computer. "Yes, his computer has been linked to our cloud. Now whenever he uses it, we'll start getting all his info. Now you, my love, get back to work and I'll work on this. See you in the evening."

I'm a bit nervous about Lisa the janitor but I try and focus all my attention on completing Neil's work. Two hours later, I'm done with the work and decide to reward myself with a coffee and a couple of Italian Biscotti.

As I turn to go back to my desk, "Hi, were you able to finish your work Miss Super-Efficient?"

Neil walks into the café wearing a skinny tee and faded jeans, his cologne filling the air. I try hard not to imagine having sex with him tonight.

"So, you up for tonight? I'll pick you at 7, is that ok?"

He comes close, raises his eyebrows as he looks at me. I struggle hard to contain my nervousness.

"Neil, I've to get back to work and yes 7 pm works for me."

I walk past him and go back to my desk, which has a red rose bouquet and a box of chocolates sitting on it. Neil walks past my desk smiling and winking at me, I smile and hand his file back to him. He nods as if amazed at the speed with which I work. I shake my head as I get back to my work.

My phone beeps. I pick it up. It's a Signal message from Carol with just a link. I click on the link. It's a tabloid report from India casting aspersions on multi-millionaire Shiv Patel's character. The report features photos of his wife and her life in India; how she was a simple girl with a wonderful character, always helpful and polite and how her life changed dramatically after marrying Shiv Patel. This is followed by details about her mysterious death in an accident. The report features how Shiv Patel's mistress had also died under mysterious circumstances a few months before the wife's death. I smile as I know that Shiv Patel will have a hard time dealing with this, especially once the Canadian media picked up the story.

Now the kid gloves are off and the battle is on. I need to play my part to the fullest.

A full hour later I'm summoned to Shiv's office. The news

report was picked up by everyone including television networks and is now trending on social media. Shiv is up shit creek. That should teach him a lesson or two about trying to intimidate me.

I walk into Shiv's office feeling more confident than I've ever been in his presence. Shiv is watching hysterical television anchors in an Indian chat show screaming about him breathlessly. Shiv looks at me menacingly.

"Is this you?! Have you done this?"

I give him the most innocent look I can possibly bring up.

"I don't know what you're talking about Sir. What is this?"

"I know this is you. I also know that you are not Nalini but Nisha Shah. The girl from the accident."

I once again pretend as if I can't understand what he's talking about. I stare at him with my oh-so-cute-and-clueless face.

"Why don't you come out into the open and admit the truth you bitch?! Why are you still pretending?"

I keep quiet, hoping to provoke him even more.

Shiv glares at me, his face is gradually turning red in anger. "Why didn't you tell me that you're a partner in an investment company with your friend Carol Smith? Surely that is information that I needed to know."

"I don't know how that is relevant to my job here Sir."

Shiv gets angrier. "It is very relevant! Why would a girl worth a half-a-million-dollars want to work in my company as an interior designer for a few thousand dollars a year?!"

"Because I need the experience Sir. Once I gain enough experience then I plan to branch out on my own and start my own interior design firm. I'd informed you about this very honestly in the interview itself."

Shiv roars back. "Stop lying to me you conniving scheming little bitch!

You are Nisha Shah. You and your friend faked your deaths and took up new identities and came back to Canada to carry out your plan to destroy me. I know it!"

This was my cue. Seeing him angry, abusive yet helpless.

"I'm sorry sir. I don't know why you've got me all mixed up with someone else. Yes, we do have a company that trades in stocks, derivatives and cryptocurrencies. It is not a crime to do so. If you're going to be abusive towards me all the time, I'd rather not be here. I've been working very hard with barely any sleep for the last two months to live up to your expectations. If this is how I'm going to be treated despite all the work I've put in then I'd rather quit. I've already received offers from other companies. It's best if I leave this job and go elsewhere to get the experience I want."

Shiv's face turns red. He knows I've cornered him into making one of two bad choices. If he fires me, he loses control over my time and I become invisible to him. Bad Choice. If he doesn't fire me then he appears weak and vulnerable to me. Again, bad choice. He screams at me menacingly.

"No! You will not quit and run away from this battle. You will stay right here in front of me, every single day. You will do all the work I ask you to do. Do you understand?!"

Shiv takes out a file and pushes it towards me while screaming, "Sign this! You want experience, I'll make sure you get a thorough experience of what it means to fuck with Shiv Patel!"

I look at the file, it's a permanent employment contract. I don't even bother looking at other details because they will become irrelevant very soon. If I succeed, Shiv Patel will no longer be around to enforce this contract. If I fail, I'll either be in jail or dead. And dead people don't have to adhere to any contracts. I sign on the dotted line and push the file back towards him. I look at him indifferently as I speak calmly.

"There, I signed it! Happy?!"

I walk out and slam the door shut behind me. I look around and the entire office is standing up trying to look into Shiv's office. Obviously, Shiv's screaming maniac voice had carried through the entire floor. I feel like yelling out my first real victory over Shiv but can't. It's best to not let the office know that I gave it back to him and now he's fighting once again to save his precious public image!

I decide to reward myself with a hot chocolate and go off towards the café. As I'm walking towards it, I notice Neil rushing towards his father's cabin.

Shiv is struggling to explain to his relatives in India that his wife's death was an accident and that nothing more should be read into it. He tries to pacify them and get them to understand that someone had played a cruel game with him to destroy his reputation. His relatives are aghast that he had a mistress living in the same house as his wife. They accuse him of hiding this fact and betraying not just his wife but her whole family.

As Shiv is trying to calm them down, Neil storms in. Neil who is seething in anger, takes the phone out of his father's hand and flings it aside. He shows the news report to his father.

"What is this? Is this true? I need you to answer me!"

Shiv vents all his anger out on his son, partly because he's in a tight corner and he had expected his son to be on his side and partly because of the disrespect his son has shown by throwing his phone aside.

Neil lets his father know with certainty that he's going to get his mother's death reinvestigated. That he's going to get all the old files reopened and if even the slightest doubt emerged about any wrong doing on his part, he would walk out of the family.

Shiv is stunned at Neil talking to him in such a direct manner. He's never seen such a decisive and confident personality in his son ever since he was a little kid. Shiv tries to calm Neil down. Neil almost breaks down in tears.

"You don't know how much I've missed mom. The one person who truly loved me and cared for me was taken away from me in such an abrupt manner. I've overlooked everything that you do. I don't even bother to find out what you're up to because I just don't care. I know that nothing matters to you more than your wealth and your name. Not even me! But this is the end Dad. If you have anything to do with Mom's death then I'll never forgive you. I will walk out of your life, this company and every-thing connected to you."

Shiv also yells back, "You don't know anything. You're an idiot. You don't even know the woman you're your following around like a puppy."

That's it. Neil lets loose a volley of abuses. "Don't you dare speak a word about Nalini. If I've got through the last couple of months of my life, it's because of her. If I look forward to a future, it's because of her!"

Shiv is stunned on hearing this. Neil storms out of the office and slams the door shut behind him. Shiv calms down and swears revenge on Nalini for making him go through this with Neil.

I SEE Neil walking out of the office floor still mumbling abuses to no one in particular. I rush after him all the way into the parking lot. Neil goes and sits in his car completely unaware that I'm following him. He shuts the car door and starts crying like a baby. I wonder what to do, then I also go and sit next to him in his car.

Neil is aware of my presence but moves his face away as if he didn't want me to see him being vulnerable. I understand his need to regain composure so I also keep quiet and give him time and space.

Neither of us says anything for the longest moment. Then Neil finally pulls me towards him and hugs me tightly. I ask him if he wanted to talk? He doesn't reply. Instead he keeps me held in a tight embrace. I feel really sorry for the man.

I think I understand him more in this moment than I ever did. He's spent most of the last decade of his life trying to prove to the world that he was as much of a man as his father. All his flings and affairs are just that; a young guy wanting to prove himself as being worthy of the love and respect that he thought he deserved. He was subconsciously trying to compete with his dad in the who-is-the-better-man-contest without even being aware of it.

I hug him tighter and ask him if he wanted to go somewhere. Neil finally exhales after what seems like ages. He lets go of me and thanks me. The expression on his face changes from sadness and desperation to one of calmness and joy. I'm really surprised at seeing him change his mood and his demeanour so dramatically.

Neil finally speaks up. "There are things about me that you don't know. And it's best kept that way. This is just some family trouble. It's about my dad."

"I understand. I was just wondering if there was anything I could do for you. I hate seeing you in this state."

"Yes, there is. Just meet me tonight. I'll pick you up at 7. But instead of my house, we'll go to the Fairmont Pacific. I really like that place and I think you'll like it too."

I hold his face gently and give him a kiss on his lips. Neil wants more but I get out of the car and leave telling him not to be late.

As I walk away, I find Carol waiting for me. I'm surprised but neither of us says anything. Both of us sit in her car and drive out of the office building. Once we're on the road, Carol asks me to pick up her phone and look at the last three photos.

"I'd set up the hidden mini cam to take a photo every three minutes."

I look at the photo of the man. His face seems familiar but I can't quite place it. Carol who is getting increasingly anxious asks me if I remember this man.

I stare at his face for a few moments then it suddenly comes back to me. He was the one who was with Shiv in the car when they came to meet Jack and pay him off.

Carol nods. Says his name is Adrian Ray, Shiv's henchman. Now it's my turn to get worried. Carol says Adrian Ray was wanted by the police when they were investigating the unusual death of Shiv Patel's mistress many years ago. He was never found. He has no fixed address, no fixed phone number. Doesn't own any assets and just deals in cash. We realise that we don't have access to Shiv's phone. Once we gain access to that, we can find out Adrian's number. Both of us decide that we needed to handle this man at the earliest possible.

SHIV CURSES HIS LUCK. His mistress had dumped him in exchange for money and a luxurious villa and now his son and relatives were suspicious of his involvement in his wife's death. He knew that he was being targeted by the little orphan girl who he should have killed a decade ago.

Shiv wonders if any of his competitors were behind Nalini Shah, then rules out that option as all his clients were still with him and he had increased his revenues in the last two months because of Nalini's efforts. He then thinks about the next option; was the Government after him? He thinks about it and then decides to talk to his political connections to help him tide over what seemed like the biggest crisis in his life so far.

As he's lost in his thoughts, his phone pings. He checks it and sees an email from Ava Q – a girl he had once exchanged contact details with when visiting Italy for work. He opens the email to find Ava gushing about him, how much she missed him and how she was dying to meet him. He vaguely remembers Ava – a young fashion model and is surprised that she's finally contacted him.

Ava had refused to spend a night with him when he had offered the choice to her. And yet, now she had sent a photograph of herself asking if he was interested. As he downloads her photo-graph, unknown to him, a software program is being downloaded onto his mobile phone. The photograph is finally visible.

Shiv smacks his lips as he sees a glamorous nude photograph of a gorgeous 19-year-old model 'dying to meet him.' He smiles at the photograph. Then calls up Edward McPherson.

Edward informs him that he had transferred the villa to Stephanie and was awaiting the abortion report before he transfer-ring the million dollars to her. Shiv instructs him to get her to sign the non-disclosure agreement as well before paying her off. Edward immediately agrees and informs Shiv that he was going to meet her the next day and would get her to do everything exactly as Shiv wanted.

Shiv then instructs him to draw up an agreement in the name of Ava Quark with all the riders and conditions that he had discussed earlier. Edward says he'll get on it as soon as Stephanie was done with. Shiv cuts the call and feels happy at the one positive thing that had happened in his life on this dreadful day. He starts typing back a reply to Ava informing her that he was really busy and didn't want to waste his time chasing someone who wasn't really serious about him. If she was serious, she would agree to all his terms and conditions and sign the agreement he would send her soon.

CAROL AND I EXCHANGE HIGH-FIVES. Shiv has taken the oldest bait ever known to man and had fallen into our honey trap with a morphed photograph and a fake email ID. Ava Quack had gotten us into Shiv Patel's phone.

We listen to Shiv talking to Edward McPherson and smile knowing that we'd already sent Stephanie fake abortion documents. Carol seems a bit relieved that we now had access to Shiv's phone. I smile at her and tell her to relax. Carol nods and tries to divert my attention and make me think about my first official date with Neil. We both know what this means and what I'm required to do.

"WEAR THIS GORGEOUS RED DRESS, it'll sweep him off his feet."

I wrinkle my nose, squint and ask her, "Are you sure, it is me who is going on a dinner date; looks more like you and why so much excitement, it's just dinner and drinks."

Carol conveniently ignores me as she pulls one dress after the other out of my closet and holds it against me with a judgmental look on her face. My bed is covered with dresses, floor strewn with every shoe and sandal all my jewellery on top of the dresser along with various hair extensions.

After what I call an extremely exhausting, exhilarating two hours, I'm dressed in a velvet red short backless dress with a deep revealing neck that is very generous in displaying my cleavage; long gold and red hangings adorn my ears, hair perfectly curled, along with subtle makeup - red lipstick to enhance my lips.

I meet Neil who is impatiently waiting in his playboy car to pick me up and he is unable to take his eyes off me.

"O Wow, now what have I done to deserve this."

I'm amazed at how quickly he's gone back to being his flirtatious lover boy self. This needs to be probed further but not now. I want today to be perfect. I've waited for this day and planned everything carefully; I just hope things go the way I want them to. We head to the famous Fairmont Pacific Hotel on Canada Place in downtown Vancouver.

We end up having a sumptuous dinner of grilled chicken, spaghetti and meatballs with garlic bread along with red wine. I ask him if he wanted to talk about what happened with his father but Neil quickly brushes the topic aside. He wants this evening to be about us and only us. I'm game for that.

I subtly allow my foot to move up his leg a couple of times. It has the desired impact and I can see that he's really restless behind the cool suave exterior that he's put up all evening.

Between the two of us, we finish two bottles of wine before we exchange looks that say-it-all-without-saying-anything-at-all. Neil pays the bill and ushers me out of the restaurant towards the elevators that take us to the presidential suite on the 22nd floor.

It is a huge room with tall glass windows, a king size bed in the middle of the room with a dresser on one side and a couple of couches on the other. Huge French doors lead to a dining area with a long dining table and 12 chairs. The ensuite bathroom is huge with His and Her sinks, a Jacuzzi tub on one side next to a standing shower.

Neil wraps his arms around me from behind and whispers in my ear as he continues to kiss the nape of my neck, "want to get wet? I know I want to."

"Why don't you change and then we can talk about our options over drinks." I turn around, give him a peck on the lips and leave him in the bathroom to change while I take a breather and prepare myself for what comes next.

The reflection of the lights and the moon on the water's surface gives it a surreal look like a silk drape shimmering as it flutters in the wind. The night is calm and peaceful but there is a war raging within me; am I doing the right thing? Do I really have to sleep with him to get what I want? I know that sleeping with him will be crossing boundaries that I didn't want to cross. I know that I'm falling in love with this sweet passionate innocent man and I hate doing anything that may hurt him and yet I must.

I guess there is a part of me that is still innocent; a part that still believes in true innocent love between soulmates. I feel my heart pounding as I continue to gaze into the darkness. I finally make peace with myself and decide that I would give myself wholeheartedly to him. That I would not hold back when we're in the moment together. That he deserved my complete self. As I calm my mind, Neil walks in.

"Hey, so what's the plan?" His arms are wrapped around me and he nuzzles on my neck while dropping kisses. I lean into him and feel him hard against me. He unzips my dress while kissing me on my neck, my arms and finally smooching me; all while gently touching my breasts. I give into the mood and go with the flow.

One thing leads to another effortlessly and I find us moving together. For those few moments our minds, bodies and souls unite. I begin to experience a high that I've never felt before. I feel his deep desire for me and know that he wants me more than anything else in the world. I let his passion rub off on me and allow myself to get enthralled in his desire for me. Soon we're both moaning with pleasure as we move faster and faster towards a mind-bending climax. We're in perfect sync with each other and reach our climaxes together. Even after we're done, he holds me in a tight embrace as if not wanting to let go of me or even the moment we shared together. He kisses me on my forehead and on my lips.

They say that a man is his most honest truest self when he's just about to climax with a woman. In that moment, there is no deceit. I have seen this in Neil today. He wants me. Wants to own me and claim me for himself. He wants to announce to the world that I'm his and his only. The intensity of what he feels for me finally dawns on me. He rolls off me, panting for breath. Both of us move away from each other and go back to being our individual selves.

It takes me time to just gather myself and get back to my senses. I turn towards him, kiss him on his chest, "well, that was... ummm, out of the world." I place my head on his chest as he plays with a strand of my hair, "do you want a drink? I know I could use one." He kisses my forehead, wraps a sheet around his waist and goes into the washroom.

Don't lose yourself in him, I remind myself. I quickly remember what I'd done all this for. I pour two drinks and quickly spike his drink. We manage to have another round of incredible sex, this time with me on the top. I smile as I light a cigarette and take a selfie with him lying naked next to me just in case I need to use it in the future.

LOOKS like the drug I spiked Neil's drink with worked well. He's been knocked out for over 2 hours now. I convince myself that I slept with him because I want to ignite his feelings for me but I know that's a lie. I'm lying to myself to just feel in control of the situation. The truth is that I love this man. I love what happens when I'm with him. I love him and hate what I have to do to him.

It's like finding your soulmate and then discovering that you have to betray him and destroy his father.

As he snores peacefully, I grab his phone and connect to the Hotel Wi-Fi whose password Carol had already texted me. I download the software on his phone, erase all traces of my being anywhere near his phone. It's almost 4 am and my work is over.

I hurriedly wear my dress, stuff my jewellery in my bag, hold my shoes in my hands and before leaving drop a kiss on his forehead and whisper, "see you at work, tiger."

As I leave the hotel I feel a great sense of guilt and regret at having used an innocent man and his honest feelings for me to get what I want.

I quickly compartmentalise my feelings for the moment so that I can remain focused on what needs to be done. I rationalise and tell myself that I need to do what I'm doing, not just for myself or even for Carol but for the thousands of girls who go through foster homes and systemic abuse. This is much bigger than me and I need to stay focused on my path.

I FIND my cab and sit in it. As it eases into a largely empty road, I look curiously at the driver who has got his face covered with a mask. He seems familiar but before I can say anything to him, he turns around and sprays what smells like a cheap perfume into my face.

Chapter Eight

S hiv wipes the sweat off his brow. He can't believe that he was stress sweating in a comfortably air-conditioned room because of a crisis an orphan girl had created for him.

He works the phone and calls every contact he has in the government to prevent the tabloids carrying news about his possible involvement in his wife's death.

Exhausted with the endless bargaining and deal making he is forced to do, Shiv wonders if the night would ever end. He has an entire PR firm working overtime to help him save his public image. Just as he and his team are able to convince one newspaper editor not to publish anything adverse about him, another newspaper calls. When he's managed to stop them, a tv news crew lands up at his office building wanting his version of the events that happened. Some news channels go live without bothering to check with him or ask for his opinion.

SHIV GRASPS the enormity of what has just happened. He was being murdered in the media, his public image was being torn apart and there was very little he could do. He's had to invest his own personal wealth into many small digital publishing houses and media companies to stop them from spreading the scandal.

It was a relentless campaign against him and all the publishers and media outlets claimed to have received anonymous tips. He knew that it had to be Nalini and Carol. Only they would fight against him with such vengeance.

Shiv had grossly underestimated the determination of a couple of young girls he had traumatised and abused. He was now paying a heavy price for it.

By the time the night was over, Shiv had stopped most large newspapers, magazines and TV channels from carrying anything about him but there were some who went ahead anyway.

It was now a deluge and he could no longer stop the news from coming out.

Shiv prayed for the best but such salacious gossip could never be hushed up. As the good people of Canada woke up and checked their social media apps – they saw viral tweets, gifs, some rumours and lots of opinions about Shiv Patel. Memes were being made about him in the hundreds. There were hashtags named after him and he was all over the news. For the first time in his life and for all the wrong reasons – Shiv Patel had gone viral.

CAROL HAD SPENT her entire night listening in to Shiv negotiating deals with everyone. Every single time Shiv would manage to buy out or convince an editor or owner to stop publishing, she would send out anonymous emails and messages to a dozen more. She enjoyed destroying Shiv's reputation.

Every single moment felt amazing to her as she remembered all the things that Jack had made her and Nal do. It was seven years of unending torture that Shiv had paid for and supervised himself. He deserved everything he was going through.

With a grin on her face Carol remembered how Nal had this brilliant idea of using tabloids and rumours to retaliate against

Shiv. It was the first of many steps that she had thought of and the first salvo had been fired. Nal had even composed a draft email meant for the tabloid media and kept it ready just in case they needed to move quickly. Her email with all the photographs and links had worked wonders and Shiv Patel had been pushed into a corner, fighting to hold on to his pristine reputation.

The pandemic had destroyed people's incomes and their savings and everyone loved a news story about a multi-millionaire and his misdeeds.

Nal had also already set up a series of draft emails to be sent out to media agencies all over the world.

Carol knew that they were ready to take on Shiv, come what may and yet a nagging thought buzzed around in her head. What if Shiv decided to retaliate in the worst possible manner?

This thought made Carol nervous and soon a lot of 'What if' questions started increasing Carol's anxiety. She quickly looked through Shiv's contacts and found Adrian. She needed to find his vulnerability and fast. She looks at the photo of Adrian Ray and at his phone number. Her reverse image search had yielded nothing.

Shiv had ensured that his henchman would never be found anywhere. She had to widen the search database.

Carol quickly contacted her hacker network. It was time to call in some favours. She sent out Adrian's most recent photograph and requested her network to find out who he really was, where he was from, what his background was – every detail mattered.

As she finished typing up the last of the requests, Carol shut her laptop and put her hands up. It was six in the morning and most of their work had gone almost exactly according to plan. Carol felt a niggling fear overcome her steely resolve. She got up to make herself a coffee when her fears turn into a real question - where is Nal?!

It was very unlike Nalini to not connect with her. As a rule, between them, they would never be out of touch for more than a couple of hours. Some text message or phone call would always arrive informing the other of where they were and what they were doing. An entire night had passed and Nal had not bothered contacting her.

Carol quickly picks up the phone and calls Nalini. The phone is switched off. Carol finds her heart beating faster. This was it! This was what Shiv had done. She immediately calls Nalini again. Again, the phone is dead. Carol goes into panic mode. She calls up Neil who is fast asleep in his hotel suite. He doesn't take the call.

Carol feels her anger and frustration growing. She knows that something is wrong. She logs into her find-my-phone app where both of them were added as family members only to find the last known location of Nalini's phone to be near the Fairmont hotel where she was going to spend the night.

CAROL LEAVES her coffee as it is, puts on an overcoat and rushes out of the apartment with her car keys. She races through the early morning traffic to reach the Fairmont Pacific in record time. She rushes to the reception and asks about Nalini only to be informed that Nalini Shah had left the hotel early in the morning at around 4am. Carol wonders what to do next.

She dials Nalini's number but it's still switched off.

Could Shiv Patel have got Nalini abducted or worse still killed?

She rushes up to the presidential suite and bangs the door only to find a half-naked, half-asleep Neil open the door. Carol asks Neil about Nalini. Neil is alarmed by Carol's sense of panic and wonders what's going on.

Carol tells Neil about Shiv's animosity towards Nalini and how he had tried to keep the two of them apart. Neil doesn't believe that Shiv would have done something too drastic to Nalini but promises to find out from his father himself.

Carol leaves in a huff and rushes back home. She had to find Adrian. If Shiv had done something to Nalini it would have to be Adrian who had executed the plan.

I WAKE up in a small dingy house that looks like a run-down hut.

I struggle to look around me and am alarmed by the eerie silence all around – the hut has some fishing hooks, some rope wire and a few empty boxes and nets.

As I become more aware of myself and my surroundings, I realise that both my hands and legs had been tied to the chair I was sitting on and that I had been gagged with a coarse cloth shoved into my mouth. I struggle to spit the cloth out of my mouth but I soon figure out that it's been tied around my face.

I look around and find that there was no one else in the room.

I smell the stench of dead fish all around and know that the driver of the cab had abducted me. I struggle to remember the face and finally it dawns on me – the eyes of the driver were a clue. I should have caught on immediately had I been paying attention. It was Adrian Ray!

I struggle to call for help but I can barely make a sound. After a dozen attempts I give up. There is only silence around me. Nothing else. This is obviously some place that's far away from any human habitation.

To make matters worse, my head feels like it's being hammered every few seconds. It must be all the wine I drank. I remember Adrian spraying something into my face. Tears well up in my eyes knowing that I was completely helpless and at the mercy of Adrian. I hate being in this state ever since I was a kid and a hate myself for allowing this to happen.

My instinct kicks in and I force myself to think instead of just wallowing in self-pity. I've taught myself to deal with every kind of crisis and this isn't so difficult. I'm sure I'll figure a way out of this.

I quickly make a mental list of all the things that would happen since the morning I went missing.

Carol would have figured out by now that I was missing. She would put the second part of their retaliation against Shiv into play and make sure that the news about Shiv Patel reached Canadian Media.

Once that is done, Carol would start poking about trying to find my location and since my phone has either been destroyed or switched off, she would try to gain access to Adrian's phone. All I have to do is be smart and I will get out of this trouble.

Think Nalini, think!

I try to control my helpless panic by focusing on my breathing and within a couple of minutes I regain my composure.

Just then I hear footsteps approaching the hut. I know that I have to play her cards right to get out of this mess.

NEIL BARGES into Shiv's bedroom without knocking to find his father fast asleep. He screams at his father and asks him where Nalini is.

Shiv wakes up startled and sees his son raging away about the kind of scum he was. Shiv tries to calm Neil down and get him to talk respectfully but Neil won't have any of it.

"Where is Nalini, Dad?"

"How would I know?" growls Shiv. He had never seen his son getting so angry and this surprises him.

"I know you've got her kidnapped. Where is she?"

"Neil, I don't like your tone. You can't talk to me like this!"

"I don't care dad. Just release Nalini and I'll be gone."

"Get out. Get out of my room! I won't tolerate you talking to me like
this."

Neil loses his temper on hearing his father asking him to leave. It's almost as if Nalini life didn't matter to him. He shouts back to his father and tells him that he won't let this matter go until Nalini is found.

"That girl is bad for you. You don't know her. She's the one who has gone and spread favours about me all over the media. She's the one who is trying to bring me and the company down."

Neil is taken aback by this accusation. Before he can begin to make sense of what his father is trying to tell him, Shiv tries to calm the situation down.

"Please sit Neil. Let me explain this to you."

Neil keeps standing, still seething in anger as his father continues.

"Nalini's parents had died in the car accident that happened about fifteen years ago. She blames me for the accident and she's out for revenge. Ever since she's joined the company, she's been creating all kinds of problems for us. The intruder who broke into my office was her. She's the one who has been spying on us and leaking information about me to the media. She's responsible for the mess I'm in right now."

Neil throws his phone towards his father telling him to look at all the social media hashtags and memes about him, the news reports about him and tells his father that he deserved everything that was happening to him.

"You're telling me that everyone who thinks you're a murderer is wrong? You're telling me that you didn't have anything to do with mom's death or even the death of that woman you were fucking in the basement?"

Shiv tries to control his anger but is overwhelmed by the rage he feels rising up within him.

"Yes. It's all lies. I'm not a murderer."

"When will you stop lying?"

Shiv once again tries to control the conversation. He tries to give a measured response despite the uncontrollable rage within him.

"I will get through this Neil. And I will overcome all the games and manipulation against me like I always have. But let me tell you this. I will not tolerate insolent behaviour from you. If you continue like this, I will kick you out of this house and your inheritance. Without me, you're nothing but a twenty-five-year-old idiot who can't get a decent job for himself. Your life and all the privileges you enjoy are because of me and I will take it away from you."

Neil also reciprocates with fury. "Go ahead, do whatever you want, but I will get to the bottom of everything. I will not have you destroy my life all over again. You killed my mother and now you're after the girl I love. She's the reason I look forward to my future again. She's the reason why I'm filled with happiness every morning. She's my hope for my future. I will not let you take that away from me. I will destroy you before you can destroy my life all over again. I will live my life the way I want. I will be with whoever I want. And you have no choice but to accept that."

Just then a maidservant knocks on the door. Shiv gets furious and asks her to get lost. The maid servant fearfully informs him that the police had arrived to talk to him. Shiv is taken aback.

"What are the police doing here?"

Neil smiles in his anger. "I have requested the police to re-open the investigation into Mom's death. They are here to question you, so you better co-operate."

Shiv looks at Neil in a murderous rage. "You will suffer for this Neil. I will show you what I'm capable of."

Neil also shouts back at his father, "If anything happens to Nalini, I'll kill you myself. I've had enough of you. So, you'd better release Nalini from whichever hell hole you've put her in."

Neil walks out of the room and bangs the door shut on his father's face.

Shiv wonders how many more problems he would have to face. As he walks out of his bedroom and enters the hall to find two policemen waiting for him, his sister Radhika, her husband

Dushyant Patel and their only son Nirmal, walk into the house demanding an explanation for the events that were unfolding.

Shiv tells the policemen that he wouldn't talk to them or answer any questions without his lawyer and promises to come to the station with his lawyers after fixing an appointment.

The policemen leave and Radhika starts asking him endless questions about everything that was going on in the media. Radhika, who is also a minority shareholder in Variety, informs him that she had sold off her shareholding in the stock market as soon as she'd heard of the scandal. She is angry at having lost half of her net worth because of the huge fall in the stock price ever since the scandal broke out. She gives him an envelope with her resignation letter from the board of directors and informs him that she had forwarded the same letter to the board of directors.

Dushyant informs him of how disappointed they were in Shiv and how the allegations of murder had damaged the family's reputation. Shiv starts yelling at them to get out of his house. Radhika is surprised at Shiv being so rude to them. The maid servant informs Shiv that the media had been calling them for a statement. Shiv shouts at the maid servant and tells her to send the media away. As he calls his lawyers and PR agents to come to his house immediately, Radhika wonders what she could do to make the most of the situation.

CAROL WAITS BY HER LAPTOP. She worries that she's using her home Wi-Fi to connect with her hacker network but she had no choice. She would have to take some security risks if she had to get Nal back and masking her IP address would have to do under the circumstances. She's couldn't be bothered going out of her house and hopping onto someone else's Wi-Fi. She didn't care about the consequences. She would find Nalini one way or the other.

As Carol waits eagerly for her network to get back to her, she gets a message in her chat room. She quickly clicks on the link provided and downloads the folder. As she opens it, she's surprised to see that Adrian's real name was Dong Nguyen, a convicted murderer in Vietnam who escaped to Singapore and then made his way to Canada.

Dong had a daughter back home in Hanoi who worked as a cook in a restaurant to make her living. Carol immediately creates a fake ID for the daughter and sends a message to Adrian hoping that he would click on the link and allow her to access his phone. She waits for a good ten minutes but there is no response. Adrian either hasn't seen the message or hasn't clicked on the link.

Carol tries to call Nalini again but her phone is still switched off. She decides to call her RCMP boyfriend Kevin Mathews.

NEIL CLOSES the curtains and darkens the hotel room before filling his tumbler with whiskey. He drinks it down in one gulp before filling it again. He needed the strength only a Whiskey could provide at this moment. Life was spinning out of control all over again.

As long as his mother was alive, he felt loved and cared for. His mother made sure that he was the center of her attention at all times and her entire day revolved around what her darling son needed.

Now that his mother was long gone, he had no one to turn to. And it was all his father's fault. He was absolutely sure that it must have been his father who had got his mother killed because she must have found out about his affairs and frauds. Neil never hated anyone in his life the way he hated his father in that very moment.

As he gulped down the second glass of whiskey, he poured himself another. Neil felt justified in getting drunk. He had nothing else to live for. Nalini would most likely end up dead like his mother and he didn't want to go to yet another cremation. He loved Nalini so much that even the thought of losing her made him want to burst into tears and cry. He knew that his connection with Nalini was real. He knew that he could have her all to himself and it was just a matter of time before he would marry the one woman he loved the most in the whole wide world. And yet she was gone!

Disappeared! because of his father. Neil was sick of his life and knew that as long as his father was alive, he would never be at peace. He wished that his father died so that he could live happily with Nalini. As he gulps down yet another glass of whiskey, he feels a burning sensation in his chest.

What if his father got out of trouble all over again using his money and his connections? What if everything goes back to exactly how things were, with his father, the dictator ruling over his kingdom while he had to struggle every single day to retain a shred of dignity.

Neil knew that people in his office used to talk about him, behind his back, as the weak son of a mighty father. He knew that no one ever really cared about him the way Nalini did. He wished he could secretly marry Nalini and end the whole problem. They could go away somewhere and start life afresh. Away from his psycho father, away from the suffocating environment at Variety. Was it even possible?

Feeling utterly dissatisfied, he opens his wallet and takes out a small plastic packet with three maroon coloured pills in it. He smiles to himself as he pops one of the pills and washes it down with yet another glass of whiskey.

Soon the burning sensation in his chest gives way to a warmness that he feels all over. It was possible. He could be together with Nalini for the rest of his life. He just hoped that Nalini would eventually be found and returned to him. Neil promises himself that if Nalini was alive and well, he would marry her and make her his own instantly – no questions asked.

That was the only way he would have the one person he could call his own.

Neil feels his mind swimming away with all the love and affection that Nalini would give him. Neil finally smiles to himself, happy with the result. He slides down the hotel bed and slumps on to the floor even as he giggles to himself. He knew that his relapse would create a world of problems for him all over again. But he didn't care. He couldn't survive another minute of being conscious of the world around him. To hell with everything. As he floats inside his head, his thoughts disappear and he feels a wonderful sensation of near weightlessness. He smiles to himself, peace at last!

I WAIT ENDLESSLY for someone to enter the hut but no one enters. I'm parched and the de-hydration is playing tricks with my mind and body. I know that if I stay calm I will be able to outthink Adrian but it's proving to be difficult. Just then I hear the same footsteps again, this time Adrian enters the hut. He walks up to me and smiles.

"Are you willing to talk? Or will you start shouting?"

I nod my willingness to him. Adrian un-gags my mouth and I start coughing and almost vomit. After a few moments I calm down and my sense of discomfort goes away. Now that I can talk, maybe I can convince him to let me go or maybe let Carol know where I am.

"Do you know who I am?" asks Adrian sarcastically.

"You're the scum who illegally entered my apartment. You're Adrian Ray or whatever your name is."

Adrian laughs, then looks at me victoriously, like a lion would look at a calf he's just pinned down.

"Good! Yes, I am Adrian Ray. And I suppose you also know what I want."

"I need water. My head feels like it will explode."

Adrian laughs again. As if my helplessness is pleasing him. He allows me to drink from a bottle lying nearby. I decide to keep drinking until I can finish the whole bottle. The more water I have in my system, the better it is for me. Adrian finally pulls the almost empty bottle away from me.

"Do you want to know why you are still alive?"

I nod. "Because you want me to admit to the world that I conspired to defame Shiv Patel with lies and fabricated stories."

"Yes. And I also want you to tell Neil Patel personally, so that he can finally see you for what you really are."

Getting him to talk to me was just the beginning. Now I need to throw the bomb.

"Do you not think that a young woman like me who can take on Shiv Patel would have anticipated all this?"

Adrian's smile disappears as he listens to me eagerly.

"I knew that Shiv Patel would come down to this at some point or the other. And I want you to know that I'm well prepared for everything you can do to me. I know who you are. I know where you've come from and all the lies you've fabricated to enter this country. I know about your family and I can do whatever I want to them. So, it's time you thought about yourself and your family."

Adrian's face goes red. He slaps me really hard across the face. My face is red hot but I put up a brave face.

"Think about it. How many women do you know who've been able to do even half of what I've done to Shiv Patel? Anyone?"

Adrian doesn't respond. He just stares at me curiously. I can see him thinking on the double just like I wanted.

"Let me tell you what's going to happen next. Shiv Patel must be world famous by now. If you check the newspapers, social media or even television news, you would know this. So, go ahead, check it out."

"I'm not going to fall for your lies. You're just an arrogant little bitch who thinks she can take on a giant like my boss."

I gesture to him to look at his phone. "Don't talk, just search for news about Shiv Patel on any search engine. Go ahead, I'll wait!"

Adrian starts searching Shiv Patel's name on a search engine. His face goes red. He looks at me and then at his phone.

"How did you...?"

"Let me tell you what happens next. If I'm not released from here in the next hour or so, the police will knock on Shiv Patel's door and arrest him for fraud, forgery and all kinds of wonderful malpractices in his company. Then, within a day or two, he will also be investigated for the murder of his wife and his mistress, something you are directly involved in. The police will hunt you down and hang you for the crimes you have committed. So once again I urge you to think about your family back home. Take as much time as you want and think about them."

Just then Adrian looks at a text message he's received from an anonymous number. He opens the message and it's his daughter trying to contact him saying that some strange people were inquiring about him and that they had beaten her up and threatened to kill her if Adrian did something stupid.

"What happened? You got a message from your family, right?"

Adrian once again looks at me. I can see the fear building up in his head.

"Go ahead, click on the link. See it for yourself."

Adrian clicks on the link. A photograph opens up with a damaged kitchen as his daughter's blurred badly beaten face.

Adrian finally loses his temper. He realises that he's the one who is captive.

"If anything happens to my daughter, I will kill you."

"If you don't release me immediately, something bad will happen to your daughter."

Adrian looks furious. He starts hitting his head. Then stops abruptly.

Then walks out of the hut and tries to call his daughter. His daughter who is fast asleep in the safety of her house has her phone on silent and doesn't take the call. Adrian yells out in frustration, then wonders what to do. He wonders if it would be wise to call his boss. He's been strictly warned to never do that but these were exceptional circumstances. His hand starts shivering in nervousness. He calls his daughter again but gets no response. He starts hitting his head in frustration.

SHIV WATCHES the drama unfolding outside his house even as his PR agent tries to address the endless barrage of questions being thrown at him.

Radhika is disappointed in Shiv and informs him that she didn't expect him to hide behind lawyers and PR agents. That he should go out and address the media and end the speculation about the murder allegations against him.

Shiv finally loses his temper and shouts at her, "Why don't you just shut up? You're no longer a shareholder in the company, so why do you care what I do? You've made your profits from the company and receive a fat salary every month for doing nothing. You shouldn't expect more than that. I want you to leave."

Radhika refuses to leave and informs him that she needed to talk to Neil first before she took the next step. She looks outside the house and sees the PR agent barely managing to keep his cool. Radhika walks out of the house and starts talking to the media. She reassures them that the police had started looking into the allegations of murder against her brother and that the entire family would be co-operating with them to address all their concerns.

Shiv seethes in anger as he knows that he'd lost control of the narrative because of a few tabloids. He knows that things would never go back to normal again even if he did manage to get out of this scandal. He wonders when the nightmare would end.

Just then he notices a camera crew filming him looking out of his window. As he quickly pulls down the curtain to hide he gets a call from Adrian. Shiv is really furious as he takes the call while shouting at Adrian.

"Why the hell did you call, you idiot? Haven't I told you not to call me?"

Adrian is really nervous at the other end and apologises to Shiv. Shiv yells at him and tells him to never call again. He cuts the call and looks at his sister trying to sabotage his life's work by claiming the moral high ground even as his reputation lay in tatters.

Shiv decides to not be a bystander anymore and walks out to addresses the media. He informs them that his sister was right and that he would fully cooperate with the police and their investigation into the baseless remarks and allegations made against him. He refuses to address any further questions and leaves with his lawyer.

CAROL BITES her nails as she drives just behind the police car rushing towards the Fraser river spot where Adrian's location had been found. She's on the phone with Kevin who tells her to stay back when they reach the spot. Carol promises him that she would not interfere in police work.

Nervous and anxious about Nalini's wellbeing, she says a quiet prayer hoping that Nalini was safe and unharmed.

Shiv Patel had done the worst thing possible by kidnapping Nalini and now he and his company would be held accountable for everything they've done. She knew the next few steps because Nalini had already planned out everything.

If anything were to happen to Nalini, Carol would send all the information they had on Shiv Patel's frauds, bribery, corruption, misappropriation of funds and illegal deals to the relevant authorities. Carol was confident that this would effectively bury Shiv and his company would most likely get suspended from the stock market.

If Nalini came out of this alive and well, then she would do the same but at a time of her choosing. Shiv Patel had effectively pressed the self-destruct button by kidnapping Nalini. He just didn't know it yet. His end was inevitable now.

Carol worried about their safety – once they did send all the scam data to the authorities, then Shiv would see no reason to let either of them live. She wondered if Nalini would agree to hiring private security? Either ways Kevin had promised to keep them safe and she hoped that he would keep his word.

AT 1 PM, Shiv walks into the police station with Louis Dean, his lawyer working with him on the re-opened murder investigation into his wife and mistress's death. Shiv is furious at the rumours in the media that he might be arrested. He storms into the Officer's room and alleges foul play. He tells them to stop spreading rumours about him and asked them what they really wanted from him?

Officer MacMillan who is in charge of the investigation sits Shiv and his attorney down in the interrogation room. He informs them that this was an official interrogation and failure to co-operate might result in an arrest.

Shiv again asks him what he really wanted? Officer MacMillan, a no-nonsense officer also yells back "This is an RCMP office, not a Real Estate deal; so now if you're done trying to intimidate us, can we start the investigation?"

Shiv's attorney Louis Dean tries to put things in order and calm the situation down. He informs the police that his client would offer complete co-operation in the matter and that they have nothing to hide. Louis Dean gently pats Shiv on the shoulder, letting him know that he had to stay calm in order to get through the situation. Shiv who has never been under such intense public scrutiny sees merit in his attorney's request but cannot help staring at Officer MacMillan in the eye. Officer MacMillan stares back at Shiv. He decides to play tough because Shiv was going to be a really tough nut to crack.

"You mistress Elma Rodriguez died at the age of 22. The official investigation at that time states that she died of electrocution in her bathtub. She was your secretary for about three months. Do you think she was stupid?"

Shiv immediately knows that Officer Macmillan was seriously offended by his attitude and had decided to put him through the a really tough interrogation. He takes in a deep breath as he answers.

"No, why would she be stupid?"

Office Macmillan smiles, "Why else would she try to blow dry her hair while still sitting in bath tub filled with water?"

Shiv replies, "I don't know."

"You don't know her, or you don't know why she would do something so stupid?"

"I don't know why she tried to blow dry her hair while sitting in the bathtub."

Office Macmillan probes even further. "Was she in the habit of displaying irrational behaviour? She was your mistress for about two years from the age of 20 until a few days after her twenty second birthday; did you ever feel that she lacked in basic common sense."

Shiv can't help but keep going with the flow of the questions. "No, she was quite an intelligent woman."

"So, you're saying that an intelligent woman suddenly did something stupid and dangerous without any precedent of such behaviour? Stupid behaviour that resulted in her own death!"

Louis Dean immediately butts in and informs Shiv that he didn't have to answer any question that he felt uncomfortable with. Shiv who is feeling insulted by the officer's behaviour doesn't listen to his lawyer, he feels the need to reply.

"I don't know why she did something so stupid Officer. Sometimes the most intelligent people are known to do silly and stupid things that can have dangerous results. I suppose Elma was one of them."

Officer Macmillan continues. "Is it true that she was pregnant with your child and you forced her to abort?"

Louis Dean again butts in. "These are just rumours. Nothing of that sort happened."

Officer MacMillan suddenly raises his voice and slams his fist on the table,

"When I want to talk to his attorney I will. If you try and reply on his behalf one more time, I'll have you evicted from this room. I want Mr. Shiv Patel to answer this question."

Shiv knows what his lawyer was trying to save him from, "No, there was no such thing to the best of my knowledge."

Officer MacMillan nods, then continues with another line of questioning. "Then why did you increase her payment. You doubled it and within a month, she was gone. Why did you do that?"

Shiv replies; "Because she was a young woman who wanted a build a life for herself. She wanted to help her family and so I took sympathy on her and gave her much more than was promised."

"That's not what Elma told her family. She wrote a letter to her mother where she clearly states that you forced her to abort. And then when she asked for more money, you got really angry with her."

Shiv tries to hide his surprise. "I was never angry with her. We had the most pleasant relationship and I was really saddened by her untimely death."

"So, you're denying that you asked her to abort!"

"Yes. As far as I know, she never got pregnant in the first place."

"Why then, did you move her out of your hidden basement and into another apartment where she eventually died."

Shiv once again feels cornered. "She was never living in my basement. She used to visit me there and then go back to her apartment."

"Her letters to her mother say otherwise. They clearly state that for almost two months, she stayed in your basement and wasn't allowed to leave or meet anyone because you didn't want your wife to be embarrassed."

Louis puts his hand on Shiv just as he is about to explode. Shiv goes quiet.

Officer Macmillan changes track again. "Do you know someone who calls himself Adrian Ray?"

"No, I don't."

"You spoke to him 38 times in the year prior to Elma's death. We have got your call records and your telephone invoices to prove this."

Shiv is taken aback. He wonders what to say, then decides to keep quiet.

Officer MacMillan continues. "Are you aware of Adrian Ray having known Elma Rodriguez?"

"No! I'm not aware of any such thing?"

"We have eye witnesses who testified to seeing Adrian Ray exit her apartment around the time she died. Did you send Adrian to kill Elma and make it appear like an accidental death?"

Shiv begins to lose his temper once again. "No, I would never do such a thing. Do you know who I am? Why would I do something like that. You are casting aspersions on my character and I will be talking to your superiors about this."

Officer Macmillan continues, "We also have eye witnesses confirming that you met Adrian Ray in an abandoned factory three days prior to Elma's death."

Shiv tries to give an evasive reply. "I meet many people for charity in the poorest of places. I don't know who they are or remember their names. I don't know the person you're referring to."

"Then are you also denying that you met Adrian Ray multiple times in the past year itself. We have GPS data to prove that the two of you were at the same location 11 times in past year and thrice in the past two months. We also have call records to prove that you two have known each other for more than twenty-five years."

Shiv keeps quiet.

Officer Macmillan shouts, "Answer the question Mr. Patel. Officers have been sent to pick up Adrian Ray as we speak. And once he is interrogated, he will reveal the truth."

Shiv's face goes pale when he hears that. Louis begs for a short recess so that he can confer with his client. Officer MacMillan stares at Shiv for what seems like eternity. Then leaves the room. Shiv looks at Louis wondering what to do next.

I LOOK at Adrian sitting in front of me with his gun in his hand.

I can see that he's conflicted. I've proven to him beyond any doubt that if he kills me or harms me in any way his daughter would be harmed as well.

So, his safest option is to save his daughter by letting me go.

On the other hand, if he lets me go, then Shiv would definitely harm him.

Shiv could get him killed any time he wanted. Adrian has a decision to make and I haven't exactly made his choices easier for him. So, I decide to help out.

"Adrian, don't think so much. You're wondering how you'll tackle Shiv after letting me go. Let me tell you this. If you let me go, I promise to take care of your daughter. I'll make sure that she runs her own restaurant in Hanoi and earns enough to live comfortably. I suggest you look after yourself and your family instead of worrying about what Shiv will do. Because I can promise you this, Shiv is finished. There is no hope for him. He will either be in jail, or he'll end up dead. I'll make sure Shiv doesn't harm you, but you have to let me go fast. Like, right now!"

Adrian points his gun at me. Then screams at me to shut up. He keeps screaming again and again as if the conflict in his head was a physical thing that would explode soon. I go quiet on seeing this. I have to tread carefully. If I pressure him too much, I could end up triggering him and end up dead. If I don't pressure him at all, then he seemed content to keep me tied up. He tries to call his daughter again and she doesn't pick up for the fourth time. Adrian looks like he's finally decided. He points the gun at my forehead. My heart stops for what seems like eternity.

I shut my eyes as I wait for the inevitable. Instead all I hear is a click and then loud laughter. I open my eyes to see Adrian laughing at me shivering in fear. If I had a gun in that moment, I would have shot him dead. I hated him so much.

Just then Adrian hears something that I missed. He quickly goes to the entrance and looks outside the hut. I don't know what he's seen, but he looks alarmed. He runs out of the hut as if he'd seen a ghost.

A few moments later, I see Carol rushing in through the entrance. I heave a sigh of relief. Carol looks furious. She quickly asks a cop to untie me and as soon as I'm free, she gives me one tight slap.

"That's for breaking the rules and being out of touch! If you ever do that again, I swear, I'll kill you myself."

I'm stunned at seeing Carol so angry. I always felt that she was incapable of showing anger. I know that this is her reaction after seeing me alive.

The fact that I'd gone missing and could possibly be dead must have scared the living daylights out of her. She bursts into tears and hugs me tightly. I hug her back. I can feel the exhaustion in her body as she literally slumps into my arms. I pat her on the back and tell her that I was alright.

That no one harmed me.

After what feels like an hour, she finally lets me go. RCMP officer Kevin Mathews is waiting for us to finish our reunion. He looks at me and nods. Then asks me a few questions about what had happened. After I finish narrating the events since last evening, he allows us to head home.

As I leave, I turn around and ask if Adrian would ever be caught. Kevin shrugs. Says we'll do our best. Carol takes out a new phone that I've never seen before and opens an app. She shows the app to Kevin and tells him that she can track Adrian as long as he continues using his phone.

Kevin takes the phone and is surprised at how Carol had access to such technology. But before he can ask, Carol whispers to him to never ask such questions and that she would tell him later in private. Kevin takes the phone and goes back to his police vehicle to talk to his team. Carol and I head home. After a near death experience I'm even more determined to take this saga to its final conclusion, but before that, some things needed to be sorted out.

As soon as Officer MacMillan enters the interrogation room, Louis begins his charm offensive. He tries to get the officer to let Shiv go because he had important business to attend. How being interrogated for so long would lead to further speculation about what was going on and soon the police would be accused of being biased. Officer MacMillan doesn't reply to any of Louis's requests. He drags his chair back and sits down. Then looks at Shiv intently.

"I have a few questions about your wife's death. As you know both the deaths are being reinvestigated on the request of your son."

Shiv tries to wriggle out of the situation. Talking to Louis had given him the confidence and he had taken the time to regain his composure. Shiv replies back, "I'm not stopping anyone from investigating what they want. I had given my statement to the police at the time of my wife's death and I have nothing further to add. So, if you could please let me go, I would be grateful. All this police business is harming my reputation and causing serious damage to my business. While I'm not accusing you of anything, I just want you to know that I've stated this on the record."

Officer MacMillan seems unperturbed. "Please tells us how your wife died."

The officer's insistence on dragging Shiv through the event all over again irritates Shiv and despite Louis's intervention when the officer insists on getting his answers, Shiv is left with no choice but to continue answering all the questions that are asked of him.

Shiv replies. "My wife died in an accident. She fell off the 10th floor of an under-construction property that we were building."

"Does that seem anywhere close to a likely scenario for you?"

Shiv begins to get irritated. "I don't know what you mean?"

Officer MacMillan says sarcastically, "Does it look surprising that the wife of a well-known construction magnate would go alone to an under-construction site on a gloomy dark day and then use the make-shift lift to the 10th floor and then fall off it?"

Shiv begins to feel his blood boiling. The officer had a way of making everything Shiv said feel stupid and childish to him. He also replies back sarcastically, "I don't think my wife knew that an officer would call her stupid such a long time after her death. If she had known, then she might have behaved differently."

Officer MacMillan shouts back, "You haven't answered the question!"

Shiv is taken aback by the sudden outburst of anger. "Then please ask me a question that I would have answers to. I don't know why my wife went there. She did not tell me where she was going. If I had known that she was going alone, I might have accompanied her. But that didn't happen."

"So, you're telling me that you didn't know that your wife used to visit under construction properties made by your company Variety Real Estate?"

Shiv tries to reply back calmly. Says "No, officer. I'm only saying that I didn't know in that particular instance that my wife was planning to visit that particular property on that particular day."

"But if you knew that she did visit your properties, then as a responsible husband, you would have advised her against going alone. Shouldn't you have done that?"

"I did do that Officer. I had told her on plenty of occasions to never visit any property alone because it is obviously dangerous. But she never listened to me."

Officer MacMillan persists with the questions. "So, let me understand this. Your wife did visit properties that you were constructing. And on every other occasion except this one, you always accompanied her?"

Shiv doesn't like where this is heading, he looks exasperated as he says,

"To the best of my knowledge, my wife has never visited any of my under-construction properties alone. I used to go with her. I don't know why she went alone this time. It's just my bad luck."

Office MacMillan knows that he's got Shiv fighting to retain control of the lies he had told the police decades ago. He continues nonchalantly, "Don't you think it's surprising that one of the owners of your company, namely your wife, visits an under-construction property multiple times and every single time she visits, she's not only accompanied by you, but also chaperoned by your chief engineer or project manager. And yet, the one time that she visits alone, there is absolutely no one with her. No manager, or engineer. Not even a construction worker. Any particular reason for that Mr. Patel?"

Shiv knows he's on the losing end. "I don't know Officer."

"Also, you're saying that you don't know if there was a reason for her to go alone? You did not fight with her? You did not have any argument with her? You did not humiliate her in front of your domestic staff?"

Shiv wonders what the officer had already found out. He keeps quiet.

Office MacMillan continues, "When did your wife find out about your affair with your mistress, Mr. Shiv Patel?"

Shiv lies. "She never found out!"

"That's not what your domestic staff of that time told us.

One driver remembers you humiliating her for questioning your philandering ways. We're getting his official statement soon."

Shiv feels like exploding. He had managed to stop the investigation the last time around, but this time seems different. It's almost as if all his enemies had aligned against him and were determined to bring him down. He wondered how he would get out of this mess. He knew that his powerful friends could stop him from getting arrested, but for how long?

Louis butts in. "Officer, my client has answered all your questions to the best of his ability. So, if there is nothing further to be done, then I'd like you to release him from questioning.

Officer MacMillan nods. Then says, "I don't want you to leave Vancouver without informing me first. I need your itinerary for the next two weeks. I do hope that you will co-operate with this investigation.

Louis answers for Shiv who is still dazed by the way his life is going. "Yes, my client will co-operate with all your demands. May we leave now?"

Officer MacMillan doesn't reply. He simply walks out of the room.

A defeated looking Shiv and Louis walk out of the room and as they are leaving, Shiv notices Adrian being brought in. His face goes pale as he knows that if Adrian cracks, he would get arrested sooner than later.

Adrian in turn is surprised to see Shiv. This is the first time that Shiv had looked so vulnerable and Adrian wondered what the cops had done to him. Had he broken down and confessed everything to the police? Had he blamed Adrian for everything that had happened in the last three decades?

The look on Shiv's face had told Adrian what he needed to know. He knew that if things got really bad Shiv would betray and sacrifice Adrian to protect his own reputation. Now he had to make a choice; should he remain loyal to Shiv or should he save his own skin?

Chapter Nine

I 'm back home and sipping my morning cup of coffee watching Carol sleeping on the couch. She's spent the entire night sleeping on the couch next to me just in case I had another nightmare.

I hope that someday I'm able to repay her, the amount of love and support I've received from her. As I watch her turn and face away from the sun, I pull the sheet over her so that she can sleep peacefully.

Being with Carol made me feel safe in a way that I could never explain. My mind wandered from one thing to another. There were so many thoughts at once. Getting close to death had made me re-evaluate everything and everyone in my life and the one person whose absence stood out was Neil. Where was Neil?

Carol was always there for me and that part of my life was sorted and remained that way since I was about eleven. But what about Neil? Carol had told me that he was in bad shape but something seems off about the whole thing. Neil had promised undying love to me again and again.

Just a couple of days ago, I truly felt and experienced how wholeheartedly he gave himself to me and yet when I was abducted, he wasn't there. I'm back home now and he's still not here. He hasn't even called. I checked my phone, the police retrieved it from Adrian and Neil hasn't bothered to check on me to see if I'm even alive. Just then Carol wakes up startled. She looks at me and sighs with relief.

"Thank God! I dreamt that Shiv had sent someone to kill you!"

I smile back at My Sister, Miss High Anxiety, "He just might. It's not over yet!"

Carol goes to make her coffee and comes back within a couple of minutes with a freshly brewed cup. "Do you really think he'll do that, especially after knowing that Adrian has been arrested?"

I reply back because I know my enemy better than Carol. "He will do that precisely because Adrian has been arrested. The only way he gets out of trouble, is if he proves that I was a mentally troubled young woman who imagined all kinds of things about him and conspired to defame him. Plus, if I'm dead and he can claim that I killed myself because of some mental illness, it reduces the problems that he would eventually have to face in court."

Carol's joy at seeing me safe and sound disappears. "So now what?"

I look determined as I reply, "We continue our fight!"

I take out my laptop and show her all the draft emails that I'd composed and kept ready for precisely this kind of situation.

Carol once again asks me to do a rethink. "Once this goes out, then Shiv might get arrested. That means it's a fight to the death. He won't hold back!"

I reply back confidently. "I'm counting on it!"

Carol says "Wait, then we must put security in place. I'm hiring two bodyguards each for the both of us. One will masquerade as a driver. While the other armed guy will always be around us, just in case Shiv's goons try to spring a surprise on us."

My immediate reaction is to say no, but I check myself. I have to allow Carol to do what she feels is right. Her hunches always turn out to be correct and I'm certainly better off with a couple of bodyguards protecting me. I agree to her idea. She picks up the phone and sends what seems like a Signal message. Then smiles at me and says "Done! The bodyguards will be here in an hour!"

I'm surprised at how she'd already set up everything before asking me.

CAROL LOOKS at me with a bit of apprehension as I look at the email I'd composed months ago. It has all the glorious details of Shiv Patel, the official and unofficial payments made to various people, the so-called consultants who did the dirty work on Shiv's behalf, details of frauds, slush funds, malpractices, everything necessary to pin Shiv down to the ground and make sure that he stays there for a long time.

Carol gives me a bear hug. I look at her and wink. Then hit 'Send' on my computer. The email is sent to all the official agencies and departments of the Government along with all media outlets including small blogs and local newspapers.

I'VE MADE it impossible for Shiv Patel to ever recover from this blow and he will soon know the mess he's in. Now time to enjoy my coffee and wait for the house of cards to come crashing down.

EDWARD MCPHERSON FACES one of two choices. Either die slowly or die fast. Ever since the news had hit the TV stations about the frauds and malpractices going on at Shiv Patel's company, he knew that he would get under the scanner.

It was just a matter of time before Shiv Patel heard of the news and called him. He was the only person who had access to the confidential files besides Shiv himself. Edward knew that he was in no man's land. If he confessed to his boss, then Shiv would make him suffer a slow painful death, something he'd seen other executives in the company go through.

If he went against his boss and confessed to the authorities, then he would go to jail and his wife and her family would kill him. Nalini had told him that once he handed over the documents, he would be out of the picture and there would be no mention of him anywhere. She had stuck to her promise and all the leaks about Variety Real Estate only mentioned a hacker's work, not a word about him. But how would he convince his boss?

Just then he hears his mobile ringing. It's almost as if the phone knew that there was trouble brewing at the other end and so it rang louder than usual. Edward takes in a deep breath and takes the call.

Shiv asks him straight up front, "Did you ever give out any details of our accounts to anyone?"

Edward takes the easy way out. "No boss, I've never shared details with anyone!"

Shiv begins growling in anger, "Then how do they know about our accounts. I thought the accounts couldn't be hacked."

Edward pleads innocence. "I don't know Sir! Someone really smart must have figured out a way to hack into our accounts and get all the details."

Shiv finally lets loose; "You fucking idiot, if a hacker got through our accounts and had access to our funds, why would they not transfer out all the money instead of doing some expose?"

Edward begins to stutter and mumble incoherently.

Shiv finally asks him one more time, if he's ever given out details to anyone. Edward feels the anger rising in Shiv. He wonders what to do. Shiv warns him. Tells him that if he ever found out that Edward had indeed passed on the information to someone and lied about it, he would get Edward killed.

Edward blurts out that he had no choice. That he was black-mailed into giving out the information to Nalini Shah.

"You're dead, you stupid piece-of-shit! You're dead, you understand that! I want you to write out your statement about being blackmailed into parting with confidential information and send it to me right now!"

Edward agrees to all of Shiv's demands. He also promises to send his resignation along with his signed confession.

Shiv who is in his bedroom, slams the phone down on him and screams out in anger. He then calls Stephanie but is informed that the number doesn't exist. He tries again and gets the same message. Shiv then asks his contact in the North Vancouver area to find out if the villa was still registered in Stephanie's name. He gets a call back within a few minutes informing him that Stephanie had sold off the property with 24 hours of it being transferred to her name. That a British millionaire now owned it.

Shiv puts the phone down. Then checks his computer to see the abortion document that Stephanie had sent them. He calls the hospital to find out if any such abortion had taken place. He is informed that there was no Stephanie registered in the patient list in the hospital's records for the last three months. Shiv laughs. He laughs at his own stupidity.

Two young girls had got the better of him. Nalini and Carol had planned everything right from the start and executed their plan to perfection. And now he was in a mess that was difficult to get out of.

Shiv then opens his hidden locker and takes out a satellite phone. He dials the only number on the phone and asks for help. He needed two people eliminated and he needed it done fast.

Carol who is listening to Shiv talking to Edward on the phone knows that things were about to get really bad. She knows that Shiv had made another call from another phone number but couldn't hear what he said clearly. She looks at Nalini who tells her that things would be alright.

Just then they hear a knock on the door.

Carol is really nervous but Nalini seems confident. It is highly unlikely that paid assassins would knock on the door and attack them in broad daylight. She opens the door to find four security guards looking at her curiously. She invites them in and starts asking about their credentials.

NALINI'S PHONE suddenly starts ringing, Carol picks up the phone to see that it's Neil calling. She informs Nalini who tells her to ignore his calls. Carol cuts the call and starts paying attention to Nalini clicking photos of all the guards, their IDs and taking down their phone numbers and other details.

Just then Neil calls again. Nalini looks irritated at being interrupted, she takes the call and before Neil can say anything, she curtly informs him that she doesn't want to have anything to do with him. Even as Neil begs for a chance to talk to her, she cuts the call and goes back to talking to the guards.

SHIV LOOKS out of his window and sees a media news van parked outside. He knows everything that would happen next and takes a deep breath. He needed to put things in place before the inevitable happened. He tries to call Neil who is still holed up in his hotel room.

Neil sees Shiv's call on his phone but doesn't take the call. Instead he pops another two maroon pills and lies down. Tears roll down his eyes as he struggles to get a grip on his life.

Shiv calls again. This time Neil takes the call. He's barely conscious and listens to what Shiv has to say. Shiv asks him if he'd seen the news. Neil tells him that he doesn't care. Shiv tells him that their company was in a serious problem. Neil puts on the TV channel in his room and watches reporters doing stories from outside their house about Shiv Patel's frauds and mismanagement. Neil laughs.

"This is well deserved Dad. You ran a listed company like it's your personal kingdom and did whatever you wanted. Now you'll face the consequences."

Shiv gets angry. He doesn't understand how his son can be so casual.

"This is your inheritance, you stupid idiot. You're going to inherit this company from me, whether you like it or not. So, you'd better get your act together."

Neil laughs again, "I just don't care. This is the second time you've destroyed my life. I will never forgive you."

Shiv is surprised. "Are you on drugs again?!"

Neil doesn't reply.

Shiv screams into the phone, "Once Nalini is done with me, she'll come after you. You're next. I hope you've read the documents I've sent you!"

Neil cuts the call and throws his phone away. He switches off the lights in his room.

SHIV GETS a call from his accounts team. Their stock had nosedived and is at a fifty-two-week low. The board had called for a meeting and he was expected to attend it. Shiv cuts the call.

He had things to do. Just as he walks out of the room, he sees his sister and her family waiting for him in the hall. Shiv asks them curtly why they'd not left yet. Radhika, his sister, screams at him.

"I've been through all the documents presented to the media. It's all true isn't it. You've been bribing your way to contracts and permits. You've been siphoning off money from the companies using fake invoices and doing frauds by the dozen. You've deprived the entire family of their share of profits Shiv. I will make sure you pay for this!"

SHIV LOOKS at her in the eye and shouts back, "It's because of me that this company even exists. None of you know how to do anything. All you know is how to ride piggyback on my hard work. Yes, I did whatever I had to do to grow the company. And I don't regret anything. How do you think I paid off all the gate-keepers? In every project we've done, we've had to pay off people. How do you think I did that? Now get out! All of you! Out!"

Radhika walks out of the house with her husband and her son. She notices the news van nearby and walks towards it.

The news crew immediately rushes towards her to get her opinion. Radhika decides to make a statement.

"I'm Radhika Patel, sister of Shiv Patel. I along with my husband and my son are aghast at the various misdeeds that Shiv has been doing in this company. As one of the founders of Variety, I completely denounce any fraud that has been done and request the relevant authorities to investigate every allegation made against Shiv. I intend to set things right with this company and I'm going to approach the board to demand Shiv's immediate resignation. That's all I have for now. Thank you!"

She looks back at the house and sees Shiv glaring at her from the door.

She smiles at him and walks away towards her car.

Shiv walks back into the house, away from the media's prying cameras and calls her. He tells her to stop talking to the media and threatens her with dire consequences if she didn't comply.

Radhika also puts up a brave front. She informs Shiv that unless he was willing to divide the company's shareholding and make her son an equal owner in the company, she would do as she wanted.

Anyway, Radhika taunts Shiv, Neil will never be able to manage the company. She asks Shiv to first find his own son and see if he was still alive or had drugged himself into an overdose.

Shiv flat out refuses and threatens her to stay away from him and Neil and the company or it would be dangerous for her and her family.

Radhika tells him that if he tried to harm her or her family in any way, she would inform the police about the way he had treated his ex-wife Alpa before her death.

"WE STILL HAVE nothing on Shiv. No one he's bribed is ever going to admit to having received money from him. He can cook up a nice little story about the fake invoices and the frauds and get away with this. This story will be hushed up in no time."

I nod as Carol speaks her mind.

Both of us have been listening to Shiv talking to his contacts, his sister and his son. Both of us know that everything we'd done amounted to very little.

At best, Shiv would be removed from the company's board and slapped with a huge fine that he would be more than happy to pay. He would then fight his way back to becoming Chairman of the board once again in a couple of years.

"We need Adrian to confess! That's the only way out. If Adrian confesses to everything he's done for Shiv, then we have something. And that is something he just won't do. The cops have been trying to break him down for the last six hours and they haven't got a word against Shiv out of him yet."

I nod, then think of a way ahead. "I think I know what will convince him."

Carol looks on curiously as I pick up my phone and make a call.

"IF YOU ARE GOING to vote against me, then let me remind you that all of you are minority shareholders. I still own 70% of this company and I will replace you at the first opportunity I get." Shiv threatens the board members who are staring at him in amazement, wondering how a man who has faced so much criticism from everyone in the media and the industry be so brazen.

WHAT COMES FROM WITHIN

The board members try to reason with Shiv. He had at first been accused of two murders and now there were serious allegations of fraud and mismanagement. He had to go and the most dignified way out, was to resign.

Another board member asked Shiv if he wanted to be kicked out of his position. She warns him that if he didn't offer to resign then the board members had the option of voting him out.

Shiv tries to threaten and intimidate them but the board members keep persisting with their request.

After a lot of arguments and counter-arguments Shiv finally concedes that the board members were doing the right thing to protect the company. Shiv looks outside the window and sees many reporters and news vans waiting for the announcement. He signs on the resignation papers, throws it towards the board members and walks out.

The board members heave a collective sigh of relief when they finally see Shiv's resignation. One of them calls for the company PR team to come in so that they could announce Shiv's resignation in the media.

THE BOARD MEMBERS then pass a resolution to elect Neil as the new chairman of the board. The resolution is passed unanimously.

Neil is called into the room. Everyone congratulates him on being made the interim Chairman of the board. Neil thanks them and requests them to co-operate with him so that he can face the investigation into the company's activities. A few minutes later, the company spokesperson announces to the media that Shiv Patel had resigned from the board and that Neil had been elected as the new chairman.

PHOTOGRAPHS OF NEIL are all over the media. Carol and Nalini watch the proceedings on their TV at home. Carol looks at

Nalini trying to figure out if she was okay. Nalini seems to have no feelings about the event.

SHIV PATEL ADDRESSES THE MEDIA. He claims that all the allegations made against him and the company were false and that he had resigned from the board so that a full impartial investigation could be conducted without any interference on his part. He claims that a malicious campaign was being done by bringing up the past so as to damage his reputation. That he had already requested the relevant authorities to investigate the source of these allegations.

Carol look at me wondering where Shiv was going with all this. She tries to reassure me, "Don't worry, unless you want to come out into the open with your identity, no one will be able to find out that we're behind this scandal."

As I ponder over my options of going public with everything that Shiv Patel had done to us, the doorbell rings. The security guard informs us that one Mr. Neil Patel had come to visit us. I shake my head in disbelief as I open the door to find Neil smiling at me. I turn away from him, allowing him the space to walk into the house. Neil keeps looking at me, it's almost as if he's been crying for a long time.

"NALINI, please don't blame me for my father's sins. I know the harm he's done to the both of you and I wanted to apologise unconditionally."

Both of us are startled at Neil openly admitting to the truth.

"I'm sorry, what did you say?" asks Carol who is curious about where this was going.

Neil looks absolutely sincere when he speaks. Carol is surprised at his openness and the remarkable difference between him and his father.

Neil continues, "Please Nalini, please don't blame me for my father's sins. I know everything that has happened. He subjected you to endless abuse and torture in various foster homes. He paid people to make your lives miserable. I know the truth. I've come to request you not to blame me for any of what has happened."

Seeing his sincerity, Carol looks at him sympathetically.

I KEEP LOOKING AT HIM, wondering how to respond to him. He is right, I can't blame him for his father's crimes. But he's no angel either. And yet, the man in front of me was different. Not just from his father but also from the Neil I have known. Something had changed.

"Where were you all this while Neil? You claimed that you wanted to spend the rest of your life with me, and yet when I was in serious trouble, you weren't there!"

Neil looks at me with hope, "I can't handle another cremation Nalini. I can't handle yet another person I love being taken away from me. Years ago, it was my Mom. My Dad got my Mom killed because she informed all my relatives about his affairs. And now it's you. I feel like my life is stuck in a loop. Every time I truly love someone, she's taken away from me. And the reason is always my father. When Carol informed me that you'd gone missing, I went and confronted my father who claimed to not know anything about you. I thought you had died Nalini. I thought my father had already got you killed. I couldn't handle it. I finally manage to find out about Adrian and spoke to him. I paid him off so that he wouldn't kill you."

I am truly surprised. Neil's behaviour is completely unexpected. I had expected him to take his father's side when he learnt the truth about me. I keep probing him, "You didn't even bother to call me or meet me all this while? Why Neil?"

Neil looks at me like a guilty child would look at an angry parent.

"Because I've had a relapse Nalini. I've gone back to doing

what I had started doing after my mother's death. I've gone back to drugs and alcohol."

CAROL IS REALLY surprised at seeing this side of Neil. She looks at me with a give-the-guy-a-chance look. Neil continues talking as if he's in a trance. He goes down on his knee, takes out a ring and looks at me with all the hope a dying man could muster.

"Please Nalini. Please marry me. This entire incident has left me shaken to the core. And I know that I can't live without you. I want you with me for the rest of my life. I promise to help you achieve everything you want. Marry me."

I'm taken aback. This is something I'd definitely not anticipated.

Carol lets out an "Aww..."

I look at her angrily and she covers her mouth with her palm to keep it shut. I look at Neil and know that this is for real. That he was genuinely proposing marriage to me. I wipe off the tears around his eyes and gently hold his face.

"Can you give me some time to think about it, Neil? Too much is happening all of a sudden in my life and I need time to think."

Neil continues with the same intense sincerity. "Do you not trust me Nalini? Did you really think that after finding out the truth, I would side with my father and defend him? Do you not know how much I love you?"

"I do know that Neil. I do..."

"Then why don't you say yes?" Neil takes out a paper from his pockets and shows it to me. It's a marriage license.

"I applied for it on your first day at work. I'd decided then that if you agreed, I would marry you. All you have to do is say yes and we'll get married tomorrow. I've already arranged for everything!"

I hate being put under pressure like this. I love the fact that Neil had poured his heart out to me, but I hesitate to decide because I don't want to make a mistake. Neil senses my hesitation. He puts the ring back into his pocket and takes out a knife.

"Since you don't trust me and aren't going to marry me, my life isn't worth living. I can't go through everything all over again. You're the only hope I have to find happiness. And if you're not going to marry me then, I'd rather not live."

NEIL SLASHES his wrist in front of us. Before I can react, he sits down on the floor as blood rushes out of his wrist. Carol screams out in fear. The security guards come rushing into the apartment. I burst into tears and cry uncontrollably. I hold up Neil's wrist and scream out for someone to call an ambulance. The security guards immediately call emergency services. Carol rushes and gets some tape and bandages. I quickly tie up the wound even as I'm crying.

"Do whatever the fuck you have to do, but I want this man out of here before the end of day today, am I clear? Don't worry about the money, I'll pay whatever I have to but he has to be out and today." Shiv shouts as Louis is getting out of Shiv's car. Louis promises to do the best he can and leaves. Shiv drives away in anger, away from the police department building as Louis goes in to meet Adrian and represent him.

LOUIS SEES MacMillan and informs him that he wanted some time with his client, Adrian Ray.

MacMillan smiles.

"Funny isn't it, you representing two criminals in the same case and yet deny that they are connected to each other. Who is paying you to represent this shit-head?"

Louis doesn't reply. He repeats his request to be given time with his client. MacMillan opens the door to the interrogation room and sees a semi-conscious Adrian. He opens the door wider to let Louis in and closes the door behind him.

Louis informs Adrian that Shiv had sent him as his lawyer. Adrian is barely able to talk. Louis knows how desperately the police wanted a confession from Adrian. Louis asks Adrian if he'd said anything to the police yet? Adrian shakes his head. Louis tells him to just hold on for a few more hours. Tells him that he would be rewarded handsomely for his loyalty and his silence.

Adrian smiles despite the pain he is in, "You're here to ensure my silence. You don't work for me, you work for Shiv."

Louis tells him not to think negatively. That he was the best chance at getting out.

Adrian keeps staring at him for a long moment. Then says, "You're here to spy on me. To make sure that I don't implicate Shiv in anything."

Louis begins to get unnerved. He knows that if Adrian betrays his client, then it's all over for Shiv. He tries to calm Adrian down and make him see things positively. He tells Adrian how valuable he was to Shiv and how Shiv had decided to relocate him, with a new formal job, a new apartment and a fat salary.

Adrian keeps nodding at everything Louis says. Then finally speaks, "Can I make a few phone calls?" Louis offers his phone.

ADRIAN CALLS UP HIS DAUGHTER. His daughter who is in Hanoi finally takes his call.

"Dad, are you alright?"

Adrian is relieved on hearing her voice, "Yes, I wanted to ask you the same question. Are you okay?"

His daughter sounds cheerful, "I have quit my job. I'm seeing up my own restaurant now."

Adrian is surprised. "How can you afford that?"

His daughter walks out of the kitchen she was working in.

She whispers into the phone, "Someone called Nalini called

me. She told me everything that had been happening there. She paid me a hundred thousand dollars to help me set up my own restaurant and told me that she would give me another four hundred thousand dollars if you co-operated."

Adrian is surprised. "How does she have your number?"

"I don't know all that dad, but I know what you and your boss did to those two girls. You ruined their lives dad. That is unforgivable. You destroyed the lives of those young women for money. Why are you doing all this?"

Adrian begins to get agitated. "I had to do whatever I did to survive. It is my boss who got me out of jail and gave me an opportunity to live."

"I know that Dad, but don't you think you've done enough? It's time to clean the slate Dad. Nalini has promised to help. She said that if you co-operated with the police and confessed to everything you've done, then she would try to get you a lesser sentence. She said that is the only honourable choice you had left."

Adrian chokes on hearing his daughter speak. "I'm sorry if my actions disappointed you. I don't want to be an embarrassment to you."

His daughter tries to console him. "Please dad. Do the honourable thing. Please confess everything to the police. Your boss plans on getting you out of police custody and then killing you. He wants to make sure that you remain quiet forever."

Adrian smiles.

He knows his daughter is right.

"I'm sorry that your life turned out so miserable Dad. But your loyalty to your boss is going to get you killed. So please do the right thing for once."

Adrian cuts the call and gives the phone back to Louis.

Louis looks at Adrian wondering what had just happened. Adrian doesn't say anything to him.

Officer MacMillan comes back into the room. He looks at Louis and then at Adrian.

"This isn't a love nest. Now get out." Louis gets up to leave.

Louis sees MacMillan and starts talking loudly, "I will be back with an order from the court to have my client released, till then make sure he's treated properly as it won't take me long to come after your team, officer."

Adrian looks at MacMillan pensively. MacMillan shuts the door as he stands tall in front of Adrian.

"So, where were we?"

Adrian looks at him pensively, "I need your help. If you help me, then I can help you."

Officer MacMillan looks at him curiously.

"If you give me two weeks. I will give you a signed written confession about everything I've done for the last thirty years. All the work that I've done for Shiv Patel. I will also read out my confession on video so that you can record it in the presence of whichever authority you want and show it as evidence in a court-room whenever this case comes up."

Officer MacMillan is surprised at the turn of events. "If you're trying to fool us Adrian, let me tell you that..."

Adrian cuts him off. "You have my word. Take me to which-ever undisclosed location you want. Just give me food, sleep and a computer for two weeks and I will write out everything I've done for Shiv including killing his wife, his mistress and another four people. I'm doing this for my daughter. I know how Shiv Patel works, I won't end up reaching the court. He will get me killed much before that. So, if you want me to co-operate, you'll have to protect me for the next two weeks."

Knight Rover, codename for one of the most successful private military snipers in the western hemisphere, looks through his night vision lens. He sees his target behind the window, covered by a thin curtain. He knows that the glass on the window would be bullet proof. He once again looks at the photo of the target on his phone. It's the same man.

An Asian man in his late fifties, a star witness in a big criminal case, who was under police protection. He looks at the wind reading and adjust his shot ever so slightly. It was a relatively calm night and he wouldn't have to adjust his shot too much. Sitting two miles away on the top floor of a hotel, he waits patiently for the opportunity to take the shot. He had one shot to kill the target, maybe two if he was really lucky.

The witness was under heavy police protection and hiding in a safe house.

He had created a distraction for the witness and waited for it to happen.

As he lights his third cigarette, he sees the food delivery guy approaching the building. The food delivery guy looks around at the building, then figures out where he had to go and approaches the target's room.

A policeman standing guard outside the room, stops him and checks the package. It was Pho, a rice noodle soup from a Vietnamese restaurant. The target is surprised at the food order and asks what it was. Once he finds out that it's his favourite Vietnamese dish, he accepts his order. The policeman asks the delivery guy to open the paper bowl and taste the food. The delivery guy is surprised but does as ordered.

Once the cop sees that the food was deemed okay to consume, he lets the target receive the packet. As the delivery guy gives the packet and moves away, the policeman hears a cracking sound and then sees the delivery guy's head explode. Before he can shut the reinforced door, he sees his star witness on the floor holding on to his bleeding leg. He immediately shuts the door and calls for medical help.

Within two minutes, a resident doctor comes rushing towards them. The policeman shuts the door behind him as the doctor attends to the witness. Knight Rover frowns. He's not sure if he managed to kill the target. He knows that he will not get another opportunity anytime soon. He dismantles his sniper gun and moves out in the quiet of the night.

SHIV SCREAMS into his satellite phone. "What do you mean you're not sure?"

He listens patiently for a few seconds. Then curses his luck and cuts the call.

Shiv sits down on his bed and exhales. He was about fifty-six years old and had taken on more stress than anyone else he knew. He was worn out. Nothing he was doing seemed to be working. He knew that he had some serious decisions to take, the first of which involved handing over the company to his incompetent son. He hated the fact that he had to do something like this in the prime of his life, but there weren't too many options left for him.

IF ADRIAN SUCCEEDED in recording his testimony on video in the presence of a judge, there was no way that he could save himself. He would go to jail for life. He didn't know what had convinced Adrian. Did that girl offer him more money? Adrian wasn't the kind who was easily intimidated. Shiv shakes his head in disappointment, then calls up Neil.

Neil refuses to take the call. Shiv sends him a message saying that he wanted to hand over ownership and control of the company to him. He requests Neil to come to the house immediately. Neil sees the message and says okay.

AN HOUR LATER, Neil walks into his house to find his father sitting with his lawyers. Neil is in no mood to talk. Shiv notices him and asks him if he was willing to take ownership of the company.

Neil looks irritated, "I will take ownership of the company, only if you agree to never have anything to do with it. I don't want to have anything to do with you, but at the same time, I don't want the whole organisation and the employees to suffer for your stupidity."

Shiv nods. He signs on the transfer documents and pushes them towards Neil. Neil quickly reads through them and then signs the agreement and two copies. The lawyers congratulate him and leave. Neil is also about to leave when Shiv requests him to wait.

"Son, can I please talk to you for a few minutes."

"I don't want to know what you have to say, I don't care about you anymore."

"I just transferred the whole company to you. It's eighty percent of my total wealth and you won't even talk to me?"

Neil laughs. "What you've transferred is a nearly bankrupt company. After all the investigations are done and the fines and damages are paid for, what I'll inherit from you is a company that is hugely indebted with no liquid cash, a completely destroyed reputation and a whole lot of angry shareholders. You can tear up this agreement and keep the company to yourself if you still think that you've transferred something of value to me."

Shiv mumbles something angrily, then looks at Neil, "Do you know why this is happening? It's happening because of that girl Nalini Shah and her friend Carol Smith. They blackmailed Edward McPherson and got all the confidential files. And what are you doing? You're busy following her around like a lost fucking puppy. Can you please see the truth? None of this would have happened if we had not hired that girl. But you insisted and here we are."

Neil shakes his head in disappointment. "Instead of admitting that everything that is happening today is your fault, you are as usual blaming Nalini. Did you not pay her foster families to keep her in control through abuse and exploitation?"

Shiv goes quiet on hearing this. He knows that Neil must have talked to Adrian.

Neil continues setting the record straight, "Yes, I read the report that Adrian had prepared. Yes, I know Nal's entire background. And frankly, if I was in her place, I wouldn't have bothered just bringing you down, I would have got you killed and ended the matter. That would have been true justice."

Shiv looks away, he knows that he's lost his son.

Neil finally delivers the body blow, "I'm marrying her Dad. I want to spend the rest of my life with the girl who reminds me of my mother. She loves me wholeheartedly, the same way mom did. She's always honest with me and cares about me deeply. I'm not going to let you say or do anything that would come between us."

Neil looks at his father for a reaction, but Shiv just walks out of the room. Neil also leaves the house forever.

WE HAVE THE MOST BEAUTIFUL, fairy tale wedding anyone's every seen or witnessed – he's outdone himself and I am the world's luckiest bride.

I'm dressed in a gold and burgundy Lehenga, a traditional wedding dress for Indian brides, hair pulled in a messy bun and covered with a net and lace veil; traditional jewellery enhances my otherwise subtle look.

"You look amazing and I can say this with outmost confidence, he'll be blown away." Carol cannot stop the tears from flowing down while I am finding it hard to keep mine in.

Neil has a limo waiting outside my apartment to take me to the venue, which I happily get into ready to start the new journey of my life.

It is a beautiful, bright, sunny day with a cool breeze blowing and spring flowers blooming amidst lush green lawns of the famous Stanley Park where the ceremony is held.

I walk towards a beautiful make shift stage adorned with lilies and baby's kiss along with red roses; a fire pit is lit in the middle and Neil stands on the right side in a gold and burgundy Sherwani; a traditional wedding dress for an Indian groom. He takes my hand and before I can come to my senses, I find myself walking around the holy fire while the priest conducts the marriage ceremony; Neil puts the vermillion in my hair to seal the deal – we are finally married and to celebrate with us are Carol, our office staff and a few of Neil's closest friends and associates but not a single family member.

"I can't wait to start my life with you, congratulations Mrs. Patel," Neil kisses my forehead as we finish with the vows and head towards a long table laid on the corner of the lawn facing the ocean, holding the best and the most authentic Indian cuisine.

THE NEXT MORNING, Neil addresses the media with the entire board backing him up. He announces that he's taking charge as the new owner and Chairman of Variety Real Estate. He proudly announces that from henceforth, Variety would work with the best standards of corporate governance going forward.

Neil also announces that Nalini Patel would be the CEO of the company and would manage the company on a daily basis with him. He introduces Nalini to the world as a highly educated topper from a US University who has managed to grow the company and bring in tremendous revenues over the last few months that she's been with the company.

With people like Nalini running the company, he was confident that Variety would do well all over again and would be the best company to work for. He thanks the shareholders for their patience and understanding. He then asks Nalini to speak a few words. Nalini thanks him for the opportunity to serve the company and the industry at large. She promises complete transparency that is so badly needed in the world.

Nalini informs the media that she intends to fully co-operate with the ongoing investigation and comply with all the rules and regulations. That Variety would be a new company soon, with a new sense of purpose and dedication to being a good corporate partner to society. Both Neil and Nalini receive a round of applause as they end the press conference.

NEIL TAKES me to our new apartment that we'd jointly bought. It was still not furnished but we'd made a promise to furnish it as soon as we come back from our honeymoon.

Neil looks around as I explain to him my ideas on the interior design.

Each room would have its own unique identity based on what we were going to use it for. Neil loves my ideas and hugs me with tears in his eyes.

I wonder why Neil is being so emotional. It's almost as if the darkness within him has not gone away.

Just when I'm about to ask him, Neil opens a folder and takes out some documents and shows them to me. I look at the documents wondering what was going on. Neil has made me the sole heir to everything he owned, his two bachelor pads, his ownership of Variety and some investment accounts. I ask him why he was doing this, what his urgency was. Neil holds my face and kisses me on my forehead. He has tears streaming down his cheeks as he speaks his heart out.

"I'm not alright Nalini. I have too many demons in my head and they will not allow me to live a normal life. All my life the only person I've truly loved was my mother. And she was taken away from me abruptly. And I'm now realising that it was my father all along. My father made me feel like a complete loser. I always came up short whenever I was compared to him and I know what people talk about me behind my back. I took to drugs and alcohol and sex. They were the only moments of relief I've ever had until I met you. You're the only person alive that I truly love Nalini. And I'm willing to give up everything for you. Just promise me that you'll always love me and remember my love for you."

I wipe off his tears and kiss him. "Don't worry Neil, we'll fight your demons together. I promise you, I'll always be there for you."

Neil nods and gives me the documents and tells me to keep them safely. I can see that he's holding back something. It's almost as if he knows what going to happen but for some reason cannot say it. I keep prodding him but he changes the topic. He picks me up and takes me to the car waiting to take us to the airport for our honeymoon. .

WE LEAVE for our honeymoon to the Bahamas. Most of my work was done and Shiv Patel would soon be in jail.

Adrian had recovered from the cowardly attack on him and would soon give his full video testimony. As soon as that was done, Shiv Patel would be arrested and would likely remain in jail for the rest of his life and that was justice enough for me because I was sure that jail would be the torture for Shiv Patel that my foster homes were for me.

On Carol's continuous prodding I decide to take it easy and just enjoy myself. I snuggle next to Neil on the flight and in no time fall asleep in his arms.

I'm in awe of him for standing up to his father and finally becoming the man that I dreamt he would be. By going against his father, Neil had proven to be the bigger man who was willing to stand up for what was right and I love him for that. It feels like a new beginning and I look forward to life with Neil.

Two weeks of heaven in the Bahamas and I just don't want to go back home – we spend the day on white sandy beaches, swim in crystal clear ocean and drink unlimited Pina Coladas.

Neil has arranged for a candle light dinner on the beach. There is an isle of tiki lights leading to a table with a silk red and white tablecloth holding two-dinner plates and champagne glasses with a candle in the middle.

A tub filled with ice and a bottle of champagne sits on the side of the table, "Oh Neil, this is beautiful. You didn't have to do it, thank you; you're the best husband who's in for a great surprise tonight."

I kiss him lingeringly before sitting down for a nice Italian dinner comprising of spaghetti with meatballs in red sauce along with bruschetta and finishing with mouth-watering tiramisu.

We take a short walk on the beach holding hands and occasionally kissing each other before heading towards our resort, "looks like you're tired, let me do the honours and carry you to your bed, my love."

Neil carries me into the room while kissing me and lays me on the bed as we continue to kiss and make love; he starts kneading my breasts while I unzip his pants and rub his hardened, erect penis.

I push him and get on top of him as I unbutton his shirt and take off his clothes – in no time we're naked and rolling on the bed; can't get enough of each other. I sit on top of him and have him thrust it inside. Soon we match each other's rhythm and climax together and I lie on him tired but satisfied.

"I'M so blessed to have you in my life, I couldn't have asked for more. I'm sorry for the life you had to live all these years. I wish I could somehow take them away. I promise to stand by you in everything you want to do. I promise to set things right."

He kisses me, rolls me over and takes me in his arms, "I'm a mess Nalini, and I want you to help me put myself back together. When I'm with you. I have hope for a future. Please never leave me."

"I promise to always be by your side Neil. What you've

already done is more than enough to reaffirm my faith in you. I will always love you. Just know that in your heart."

Neil looks at me, wondering if should unburden his heart. I nod, asking him what the matter was. "I need to tell you something just to be completely honest with you."

He pulls me closer to him and kisses me before engulfing me in his arms. I turn towards him.

"Dad and I had been driving home after having a nice dinner together, when suddenly, I insisted that I drive – I was 10 at the time and we had lost mum recently, so dad indulged me and agreed to it. There was no traffic at the time and the roads were completely empty. It was raining heavily and I could barely see and, in an effort, to control my enthusiasm on the steering wheel, I somehow lost control and instead of braking pushed the accelerator, which resulted in us jumping the light and slamming into a car on the intersection which resulted in the death of two adults. Those two adults were your parents, Nalini. Your parents died because of my mistake and I hope that you will forgive me for that. I was just a little kid and I made a serious mistake."

NEIL LOOKS AT ME, while I sit dazed with what just hit me. How could I be so stupid; how could I be so blind and now here I am married to the person responsible for the death of my parents. I don't know what to feel, how to react.

Neil holds my hand. I push it away. I'm furious with him and shout at him, "Why didn't you tell me all this before our marriage? Why tell me now?"

Neil looks at me sincerely. He blurts out. "Because I want to get you justice. And I promise you I will. You can give me whatever punishment you want and I will gladly accept it. And I will make sure that Dad suffers for what he's done."

I keep staring at Neil to get a grasp of what was really going on inside his head. As he rambles on and on trying to justify his behaviour, I now see him for what he really was.

"You're a coward Neil. That's what I've come to realise. You're just a coward who can't even be honest with his wife. All you had to do was tell me the truth and you couldn't even do that. This marriage is based on a lie Neil and I won't accept that. I'm sorry but this won't work out."

Neil tries to pull me closer and convince me. "I will make things right Nalini. I'm not a coward, I promise you."

"But you are Neil. You've spent your entire life playing victim. First you were a victim who needed everyone's approval and sympathy because your mother had died. Then you played a victim needing everyone's sympathy because your dominant father had become unbearable. And very soon, you'll start playing victim again because of me. You'll find some or the other excuse to play victim."

Neil bursts into tears and starts crying. "I... I don't do that. I don't need anyone's sympathy!"

"But you do Neil. You're always looking for the easy way out. You could have manned up and told me the truth about the accident. But you didn't. you're telling me now, two weeks into our marriage. I'm sorry, this marriage is over. I can't stay married to a coward who can't be there for me. You're just a child who needs everyone around him to mother him and I can't do that for you."

I GET up and start packing my bags as Neil keeps pleading with me to stay back. I refuse and leave the room. Neil keeps crying.

Then after a few moments of sitting alone, he rushes towards the bar and pulls out the whiskey bottle.

He takes out his pills and swallows all of them at one go, then pours himself a glass full of whiskey and gulps it all down.

Then pours himself another glass of whiskey and swallows that as well. Within minutes, he's in dreamland again.

The only place where he's at peace with himself.

Chapter Ten

As I wait near the hotel gate, for my security guards to arrive with my car, I hear a loud cracking sound. I look around and see the flower pot next to me explode.

Before I can make sense of what was happening, I hear another cracking sound, this time much closer to me.

The security guard who is now standing beside me, swings into action and grabs my hand, pulls me behind the gate of the hotel. He alerts the other security guard in the car. Now both security guards cover me and hide behind the wall of the hotel compound.

One of them keeps waiting for another shot, gun ready in hand to take out the assassin. As soon as the third shot is fired in my direction, he leaps out from behind the wall and starts shooting. He empties out his gun at the assassin and then comes back to get me. Both guards ensure that I'm safe in the backseat of my car as they race towards the airport.

I call Carol and inform her of what had happened. Carol tells me to check if I'm injured. I look around and see blood oozing out of my hand and left shoulder. Carol is alarmed. She tells me to get to Vancouver as soon as I could. Dazed and disoriented, I decide that I will not rest until I put Shiv in jail or ensure his death.

I had let myself get carried away by the thoughts of love and romance and Neil's passion for me. No more. Neil would have to take responsibility for his actions and would suffer the same fate as his father.

CAROL WALKS into the hospital room to check on me. It's been 48 hours since the attack on us and I'm back in Vancouver.

Except for some small gashes that have now been bandaged, I don't have anything to worry about. Carol then looks hesitant. I ask her what's wrong? Finally, after much coaxing she says that Neil had died by suicide in the hotel room. He had a serious drug overdose and died in a massive heart attack the next morning.

I feel sad for Neil but I stand by my decision of leaving him. The circumstances of his life had just made him weak and he had never developed the strength to fight back and reclaim his life. You can fight destiny only with character and unfortunately Neil was not going to win that fight.

As Carol and I go to get my discharge papers from the hospital administration, a nurse tells us that we were really lucky because if the bullet splinters had hit me on my stomach, they would have seriously injured my baby. Both Carol and I are surprised to find out that I'm pregnant. Carol asks the nurse for the scans and she gives us the file.

Both Carol and I watch in amazement at the tiny dot inside my belly. I have tears in my eyes as I look at Carol who is over-joyed. She can't believe that she's going to be an aunt and starts fussing over me. She tells me that she's never going to let me out of her sight.

Back home, even as Carol is fussing over me to not exert myself, I decide to stay focused on the task at hand. Let's do one thing at a time. I open her laptop and open the spyware app. I see only one location pin this time – Shiv Patel.

SHIV RACES his car down at full speed. He rushes towards the airport knowing fully well that in a couple of hours the police would issue a lookout notice on him and then it would be impossible for him to escape.

In the last month, his life had got totally destroyed. First the allegations and rumours about murdering his wife and mistress, then the scandal about corruption and fraud and now finally Adrian's videotaped admission of all the crimes he's committed on Shiv's behest. He didn't understand how Adrian had survived, but was later informed by his source in the police that Adrian had to wear a bullet proof vest at all times and that is what had saved him.

After a week in hospital Adrian had given his full confession to the police.

The evidence against him was damning and Shiv knew that if he got arrested, he would never get out of jail.

What made matters worse was that his own son Neil had turned against him and was now dead leaving all his wealth to his wife – Nalini Shah.

He had been systematically destroyed and he knew it. In some sense, he even admired Nalini. He knew that if Nalini had played by the rules, she would never have found out on him. Shiv had been careful and systematic but Nalini had outsmarted him and planned everything beforehand. Now she had succeeded.

Shiv realised that his game was up and so, had paid his influential friends and arranged for an escape from Canada. This was the only thing left for him to do. He could not go to Jail after the life he had lived. Just the humiliation would kill him.

Shiv calls his pilot and tells him to be ready as he was just a few miles away from the airport.

As he races ahead, he gets a call on his phone. He takes the call. It's Nalini Shah. Shiv tells her that it isn't over yet. That he would not rest until he had destroyed her. Nalini laughs. Says do you really think that I'm going to give you another opportunity to attack me?

Before Shiv can figure out what she means, he sees two police cars chasing him in hot pursuit. He speeds up trying to get to the airport as fast as he can but then sees the entire road barricaded in front of him.

It's almost as if Nalini Shah knew what he would do before he did it. He slows down his car and gets out of it. He raises his hands in the air and lies down flat on the road. RCMP Officer Keven Mathews handcuffs him.

Officer MacMillan walks up to him and looks at him angrily.

"You tried to kill one of our witnesses while in our custody? Big mistake! No one fucks with the RCMP."

Shiv is taken away by the police.

NALINI AND CAROL watch the live feed of Shiv being taken away by the police. They exchange a high-five.

Carol exclaims, "Finally the saga has ended!"

I'm still numb at how my life has played out. I suppose it is true that life is what happens when we're busy making other plans. This wasn't exactly what I'd wanted, but I suppose it's for the best.

Carol hugs me and says, "Now can we please move on to the next phase, it's the most exciting one of our lives, something I've been waiting to do for a long time."

I nod. It was indeed the most exciting phase of our lives.

I take over the functioning of the company since I'm now the owner and the chairperson. In a company town-hall, I announce that I was transferring ownership of the company Variety Real Estate to a charitable trust called "Daughters of the World."

Every year, half the profits from the company would be used by the trust for charitable purposes. This is met with a huge round of applause.

I request all the employees to stick with the company. I promise them that we would work through the tough financial situation in the company and emerge successful at the end. That all their delayed salaries would be paid in full and with interest. This is met with an even bigger round of applause.

The employees, most of whom I've known personally feel a great sense of relief that I'm in charge of the company now. I'm overwhelmed as I see a huge wave of employees giving me a standing ovation for well over ten minutes. I promise to fulfil my responsibilities in the company to the fullest extent possible.

Carol convinces me to announce this in the media. I agree hesitantly.

"Good Morning and Welcome to Vancouver Now, I am your host Kathleen Hunt and today our Guest is the CEO of Variety Real Estate, Nalini Patel. Nalini has a fantastic story and she has agreed to share it with us in detail today.

Nalini will also answer questions from the audience, in the studio and over the phone line, so, let's get started...."

A young, vibrant and very confident Kathleen sits across from me wearing a nice soft pink office suit and jacket – I try hard to hide my nervousness but it doesn't take long for her to notice my constant foot tapping and fidgeting, "Relax, it will be just fine; think of the Camera as your best friend and just talk freely."

In five seconds, before I even know it, we are on air and Kathleen shoots her first question, "Nalini, in all these years, since you lost your parents, growing up in a merciless foster system and then an eventful marriage, your husband's suicide; life has been nothing short of a roller coaster for you...what would you say to young girls and women who are face similar abuse and trauma at the moment as we speak?"

I face the camera with a smile, "Kathleen, thank you for having me on your show. All I want to say to your audience and especially young girls and women at risk, is to take control of their lives. Nobody should ever underestimate a woman or take decisions for her. As women we must always be in control, try to be just and fair to everyone in your life and finally, I think, one should always own up to who you are and what you've done. Those who don't own their lives, end up getting owned by someone else."

Kathleen asks the next question. "What is it that makes you want to stand up and fight again and again? How do you cope with adversity?"

I take a deep breath as I consider the question. Then pull myself together and answer, "I have led an eventful life. It's been filled with tremendous ups and downs and over time I've learnt to cope with it. The one thing that keeps me going is that I've dedicated myself to a cause much larger than myself. I know that if I succeed I will also pave the way for thousands of young women around the world to be free and reach their potential. Knowing that there are so many young girls out there who are struggling with life and abuse, looking for a way out and that perhaps I can help them, fills me with an energy and purpose. And yes, I've had help from my best friend, my sister and the only person who has shared my journey with me – Carol Smith!"

Kathleen asks Carol to join us in the interview and introduces her to the audience, "Carol Smith... welcome to the show. You met Nalini at the foster home when you were also a very young girl and have always stood with her through thick and thin. You have been a constant support and strength for Nalini."

Carol smiles and sits beside me as Kathleen continues with her questions, "You have shown commendable strength and fortitude throughout your troubles and it's been such an inspiring journey. You proved that it is possible to achieve what you aim for, if you have the will to do so. Nalini, now that you're the CEO of the largest real estate company in Canada, what are your plans for the future?"

Carol and I exchange looks and smile, I reply slowly and thoughtfully, "As you know Variety Real Estate is owned by the 'Daughters of the World' Trust. This Trust has been created to fulfil our shared vision of making the world a safer place for women, especially young girls."

Carol joins in, "We plan to work with advocacy and self-help groups with a focus on victims of abuse. There are many more Nalini/Nishas' and Carol/Emmas' alone and afraid out there in the world, who need help. We'll be doing everything we can to empower them and set them free. Abuse must be fought, and today we have the tools and the money to fight it. This is just a beginning, we have a long way to go and much more work to do to make the world a better place"

As we end the interview and are leaving the station Kathleen Hunt sees us off and assures us help and a platform. We get into the car and Carol's phone pings. She quickly opens her phone and sees a message from her hacker group. It's a photograph of a young girl who has been missing for a week. Carol fills me in on the details and I say, "Let's get started…".

Acknowledgments

To everyone who believed in me and encouraged me throughout this incredible journey of writing my book, a huge thank you.

Mom Jasbir Kaur Bawa for always having faith in my abilities and being my greatest critic.

Shagun Bawa and Shireen Sethi for being brutally honest with me and forcing me to convert what was a small writeup, into a fiction book.

Swaraj Bakshi for being my biggest strength and supporting me to realise my dream.

My publisher - Vincent Varghese and Destiny Media for believing in my story and helping me realize my dream of seeing my words in print.

Words can't express how thankful I am to Vincent for his guidance and support without which this book wouldn't have been possible.

About the Author

Sonal Bawa Bakshi is a contemporary Romance fiction writer who started penning poems at the age of 10. This is her first attempt at fiction writing.

A working professional by day, novelist by night, Sonal obsesses over her characters to the extent that her moods mirror theirs.

When she's not writing, she can be found wandering around the house with a duster in hand.

Now based in Vancouver, Canada, a country she calls home, Sonal is journaling about her experiences as an immigrant.

Also by Destiny Media

New Hunters at Imperial Guest House

The Day That Nothing Happened

Someone Oughta Make A Movie On This

Love Stories: My First Love

Made in the USA
Monee, IL
05 June 2022

97511115R00125